THE GUNMAN AND
THE ANGEL

Beautiful Mandy Lee enjoys an elegant and genteel life in North Carolina, but hides an unconventional past. Raised by gunfighter Dan Quint, Mandy is quick on the draw and harbours a burning need for revenge against Monte Steep, the man who murdered her family. And when she learns that Dan, who has his own reasons for hunting Steep, has finally tracked him down, she has to decide whether to forego her life of luxury and her rich fiancé to rejoin him on his quest for vengeance.

GEORGE SNYDER

THE GUNMAN AND THE ANGEL

Complete and Unabridged

LINFORD
Leicester

First published in Great Britain in 2018 by
Robert Hale
an imprint of The Crowood Press
Wiltshire

First Linford Edition
published 2020
by arrangement with
The Crowood Press
Wiltshire

A catalogue record for this book is available
from the British Library.

ISBN 978–1–4448–4598–3

Published by
Ulverscroft Limited
Anstey, Leicestershire

Set by Words & Graphics Ltd.
Anstey, Leicestershire
Printed and bound in Great Britain by
T. J. International Ltd., Padstow, Cornwall

This book is printed on acid-free paper

*For my Granddaughter Jessica,
the inspiration for Mandy Lee*

PART ONE

MANDY LEE

1

Dan Quint rode through New Mexico Territory but was still miles out of Santa Fe. He'd been camping in the open plain and now rode west along the banks of the Pecos River, about halfway between Santa Fe and the Texas border. He remembered pushing longhorns across the Pecos with Shorty Kendrick and Isom Dura throughout that first trail drive in '65 — about six years before, when he was just a pup, barely over twenty.

Willows, pines, and cottonwoods surrounded him. The air was damp, but there'd been no rain all day. With the sun down to dusk, he had shot a big rabbit with the Henry — near blew the head off — so he had something to eat after dark when he got settled. He found a five-foot high overhanging rock covering fifteen feet in case rain came down, with plenty of grass along the bank. He didn't worry about Rowdy leaving him or somebody trying to steal the buckskin. The horse would make so much noise, Dan could gun the thief down before he got five steps. He set up camp with the saddle and his bedroll. He fed Rowdy a couple handfuls of oats and let him graze the grass and drink river water while the fire at the edge of the overhang cooked the skinned and dressed rabbit. Above the crackling of the fire, he heard the river, something never possible before with the bawling of Texas longhorns.

'Hello, the camp.' A man's voice came from the trees.

Dan felt a stitch of surprise. He stood with the Colt in his hand, then knelt and backed under the overhanging rock. 'Say yourself and move in the firelight with empty hands.'

'Clyde McCabe, Deputy Marshal.' The man stepped out of the trees with palms out. 'Mean no harm to a lone rider.'

Firelight flickered on his stubbled face that looked hacked from granite, his Montana Peak Stetson tattered and torn at the corners. He wore a Colt cross-draw stuck at his belly in a cartridge belt. His face and body shifted, willow lean and easy moving — about thirty. The badge shone.

'Step in,' Dan said, holstering the Colt. 'I'm Dan Quint.'

'I'll move on if you say. No wish to bother.'

Dan said, 'Bring in your horse. I got a good-size rabbit roasting, warm beans, and hot coffee. Enough for two if we ain't hoggish. I can use the company — been riding lonesome since Abilene.'

After McCabe's saddle and bedroll were spread on the other side of the campfire from Dan's, the two men set to on rabbit and beans washed down with hot, strong coffee. They saved conversation for after the meal. While Dan cleaned up, Clyde produced a pint bottle of whiskey.

'Got something to lace the coffee and

5

take the chill off.'

Dan nodded, and as host, figured he'd be first to get information.

Clyde said, 'Deputy Marshal of Rio Gila City. We had a posse took off after some bank-robber killers a month ago. Volunteers had to leave the posse; get back to farm, business, women, whores, wife and family — things men can't stay away from more'n a month. Town marshal went back with them, said he'd recruit more to join us. Me and a couple boys stayed out, tracked the killers to North Bend then up along the Santa Fe. A week ago, we run onto them, and my two fellow deputies got gunned down in an exchange, three miles off the trail. It headed back south toward Texas and the Mexican border. Now it appears to head west.'

Dan listened with interest. 'Five men?'

'Four now. I caught one through the neck.'

'Know who it was you hit?'

Clyde shook his head. 'He carried

two Colts and a backup Derringer in his vest, fancy dresser, bowler hat.'

'Shaved head?'

'That's him.'

'I heard he's called Three Gun Baldy.'

'In Rio Gila City, they killed a teller and another deputy, Dode Chittim. They pinned me down and got away, but I managed to wound another jasper. In Santa Fe, I wired the marshal back in Rio Gila City, wrote him about what happened to the other two deputies, and the bandit I shot. I meet him and seven new men in Sierra Vista.'

'Anybody get a good look at them?'

'They wore bandannas. Just the eyes, the leader's eyes.'

'One brown, one gray.'

'That's them.'

'Monte Steep,' Dan said.

'The outlaw bandit? We kinda figured that.'

'I'm after him myself.' Dan slugged down a swallow of coffee. 'He rustled some cattle he shouldn't have.'

7

'We don't know who it was I wounded at the bank.'

'I hear tell it was Tom Baily.'

Clyde stared across the campfire. 'That one I never heard of or seen before.'

'I just know of the four.'

Clyde raised his knees and rested his forearms on them. 'You come originally from Abilene?'

'Across the plains.'

A period of silence followed.

The deputy looked hard at Dan. 'You got some Injun?'

Dan nodded. 'Quarter Cherokee, on my ma's side.'

Clyde squinted, his face a mass of tiny wrinkles in a granite slab. 'You're Deadly Dan Quint. I heard of you from down San Antonio way.'

'A lot of wild stories going around.'

'You put the word out you looking for Monte Steep a long time now.'

'Yes.'

'Got to be for more than cattle rustling.'

'It is. He dry-gulched my brother seven years ago. Been on his trail ever since. Sometimes, I lose the trail but so far I managed to pick it up again.'

Clyde finished his coffee. 'You're dead set after Monte Steep?'

'I am.'

'The Federal Poster is up to a thousand dollars now.'

'You don't say?'

'Good incentive. A man can buy a house with a little piece of property for that. Maybe attract a wife.'

'I don't need no more incentive.'

Clyde moved to his saddle to stretch out. 'You're welcome to ride along, Deadly Dan Quint.'

'I might for a bit.'

'Me and the marshal back in Rio Gila City figure on a split for that poster reward.'

'I got no interest in poster money. For me, this ain't about money.'

'It's always about money, Dan,' Clyde said.

'You'd brace the marshal for it all?'

'Or him, me. I should have been marshal, and he knows it. He may not show with any men.'

'You mean nobody could be coming?'

'Could be just you and me in a showdown with them four. The marshal already has what he wants in town. I had a woman, adorable little thing from back east, was going to be my wife. When I became marshal, we was to be married. Gene Mount come along with the happy smile, glad handing, buying fellas drinks, sweet-talking Josephine. He had personality.'

Dan said, 'He got the job and the woman.'

'I think Josephine would have been impressed with me if I was marshal. She went with the badge. I ain't a big talker, not much personality.' Clyde sighed deeply with a catch in his throat. 'And he might figure a way to cheat me out of the poster reward, in case we get that Monte Steep desperado.'

'Steep is slippery,' Dan said.

Clyde shifted position. 'You got

somebody waiting for you in Abilene?'

'A saloon owner.'

'She a good woman?'

'She's sure good to me. Spoils me better than a cowhand deserves.'

Clyde squinted, his granite features sharp in the firelight. 'Do you trust her? I mean, you trust her around other men?'

'She knows about men. But, if she chooses some other fella, I got no say.'

'A slick-talker might put a hand on her back and sweep her right off her feet.'

Dan smiled. 'Could happen, I reckon.'

Clyde watched the fire. He scratched under his arm and shook his head. 'Ah, I'll never find another sweet Josephine.'

Dan pulled the makings for a smoke. 'Life is full of surprises.' He tossed the pouch to Clyde. They stretched back on saddles. Under the protection of the overhang, they smoked and watched as gathering clouds beyond the rocks blotted any stars.

Clyde said, 'Surprises? Where you figure the trail is leading?'

'They'll stay away from towns.' Dan drew on his smoke. 'They still got bank money on them. They might head back across the Rio Grande.'

'You followed 'em to Mexico before?'

'I have.'

'Don't know if my fellow deputies will cross the border.'

'Won't matter,' Dan said.

Clyde inhaled and eased the smoke out. 'Might be just you and me.'

'I always figured to pull down on them alone.'

'No telling what might happen when we catch them varmints,' Clyde said.

'No telling.'

'As you say, Dan, life is full of surprises.'

2

Wearing slickers, Dan Quint and Clyde McCabe rode through heavy mist into Arizona Territory. The outlaws ahead of them apparently weren't concerned about pursuit any more. Puddles formed in desert hoof prints made the trail easy to follow. Four horses moving toward Tucson. Mist thickened to hard rain. They didn't talk, but rode walking horses beside each other, their heads bent, the rain washing off their Stetsons and slickers. Looking up now and then, they were ever mindful of ambush.

The trail curved southwest, away from Tucson. Monte Steep and his gang were sure enough headed for the Colorado, then maybe south. Dan didn't want to cross back into Mexico — the last showdown had left him shot to pieces. Tom Baily, wounded, likely slowed them down. Dan figured to pick up the pace, maybe catch them before they reached the river and got into Mexico. As rain eased, he saw something different in the sand.

Hoof print puddles of only three horses, sand prints sprayed forward, horses spurred to a run.

Dan said, 'They know we're back here, Clyde.'

'We ought to split?'

'Foothills ahead — good place to ambush. One of them might have circled back. You cut right here. I'll ride ahead and come in from the front. That work for you?'

Without hesitation, Clyde heeled his mount and turned to the right. He galloped fast, his body in rhythm in the saddle, past prickly pear cactus, saguaro, mesquite, sagebrush and tan wet prairie grass. Ahead of him a mesa rose then flattened to ragged rocks, blending up to hills. Clouds broke into bright sun against desert blue sky. Rowdy ran past and ahead of the mesa, then turned for a break in the cliffs

14

leading to rocky hills.

Dan heard a rifle shot.

Clyde never made it to the cliffs. His horse somersaulted and bounced against low surface rocks, its head twisted at an odd angle. Clyde vaulted twice and rolled once. He lay still.

By then, Dan had passed the mesa. He ran Rowdy between rocks of the foothills. He pulled the buckskin up and swung out of the saddle taking the Henry with him. Over the top of the rocks, Dan saw Clyde push to his feet, then pull a rifle from the saddle scabbard, but it came out in two pieces, busted by a boulder.

Clyde got the Colt in his hand, looking at his still horse. Another rifle shot rang out from the hills. Clyde flew around to his right and grabbed his shoulder. He dove behind his fallen horse. A rider on horseback came out of the foothills, running his mount, standing in the stirrups, rifle to his shoulder. In sunshine, waist-length hair flowed behind him like a flag from under a bowler hat. His body was thick.

The only gang member Dan could figure was Louisiana Tex. Dumb move to ride out of protection but maybe Tex figured Clyde was about done and rode out to finish him off. Or maybe he just wasn't very bright.

Clyde fired his .44 but didn't have the range yet for accuracy. Tex kept coming, ready to fire.

Dan braced himself against chest-high rocks, aimed the Henry carefully and squeezed off a shot. The stock bucked against his shoulder. The echo blast ricocheted across the desert, immediately followed by another shot. Tex rolled back out of the saddle over the rump of his horse. Clyde jerked from his feet and fell back, his tattered Stetson flying from his head. Tex had fired an instant after Dan.

Dan scrambled down rocks and jumped into Rowdy's saddle. He ran the buckskin out of the hills beside the mesa and at full gallop toward Clyde. The Henry was back in its scabbard.

Tex had gotten to his knees, both hands over his bleeding chest. His horse had run out of sight. Dan came clear of the rocks and turned to ride straight for him.

Clyde began to move. He rolled to his side and reached out for his .44.

Dan unhooked the thong and pulled his Colt. He squinted with gritted teeth, not knowing if he would make it. He was within fifty yards, riding up on Louisiana Tex.

With his rifle out of reach, Tex slid one bloody hand from his chest to pull a revolver. He aimed at Clyde; fired, missed, fell forward to his elbows. He aimed again, fired, missed.

By then, Dan was close to forty yards. He fired and hit Tex in the right leg. Tex rolled to his back then continued to his stomach.

From his side, Clyde fired his .44, but the blood from his head wound was blinding his vision. The slug hit Tex in the shoulder.

Tex fired at Dan, and missed. He

turned his revolver and fired again, hitting Clyde through the nose.

Dan fired, the slug tearing through Tex's temple. His head jerked as he rolled to his back.

Clyde's head dropped, frozen in death.

Dan eased Rowdy to a trot and turned toward Clyde. Sudden silence washed across the desert. Clyde's horse lay still with a broken neck. Off the buckskin, Dan bent to Clyde. There was no face, no life, only blood oozing from wounds. Dan walked over to Louisiana Tex. He saw a hand move, reaching for the Navy Colt .36. Eyes blinked, the forehead frowned. The air cracked with a gunshot as Dan shot the man through the heart.

He'd be left for the buzzards.

★ ★ ★

Dan needed most of the next morning to pick up the trail again. He had buried Clyde McCabe in a rock grave

18

close to the foothills. There had been nothing in the pockets of Louisiana Tex as to Christian-name or next of kin. Dan slipped the Navy Colt and Clyde's pistol into his saddle bags. He tied Tex's rifle along Rowdy's left stirrup. All Clyde had was the picture of a beautiful woman with curly, dark hair to her shoulders and the name, Josephine on the back. Another man's wife, married to the marshal of Rio Gila City, Gene Mount — Clyde's rival for many things. Dan pondered if Josephine would care that Clyde was dead.

The trail headed toward the Mescal Mountains and the Rio Gila River west of Tucson. Hard to tell where they were headed now — maybe not Mexico, maybe to Yuma City and across the Colorado out California way — new territory for bank robbery and killing. They had slowed the pace again. With the gunshots, they might figure everybody ended up dead. Nothing to worry about. Louisiana Tex had seen Dan with the deputy but wouldn't have had time to tell Steep the cowhand was back on the trail. To Steep, the shooting meant Tex was probably wounded or dead after dry-gulching the deputy. The rest of the marshal's posse was back in Gila City. Louisiana Tex would either catch up or end his life in the desert.

There were three now; Monte Steep, Big Nose Rox Levant, and the wounded Tom Baily. Tom's wounds couldn't be too bad. The trio was moving along well. Dan had no personal grouch with Tom Baily. The man hadn't affected him personally. The other two were going to die because they had to. Tom might have to because of association.

Dan followed the westward trail all day and into the night. He rested Rowdy for short periods, ate jerky, sipped water from his canteen. There were plenty of rabbits, but he didn't want the noise of a shot. Let them think everybody was dead. Desert remained desert with misty mirage hills on the horizon, but mostly he passed table-lands of the flat mesa with cliff sides.

The outlaws stuck to the course of the Rio Gila River. They bypassed Yuma City and kept southwest toward where the Rio Gila flowed into the Colorado River. Dan had heard of a ferry across the Colorado from Yuma City to California. Maybe they might wait for a heavy rain — double back to cross at night. Dress heavy.

On a bluff, Dan watched a Conestoga wagon cross his path a quarter mile ahead, headed west, directly from Tucson. A wagon alone, pulled by two black mules, still twenty miles out from the Colorado, making for the ferry and the river and California — or, just headed to Yuma City. He saw a family of four, Ma on the wagon seat, Pa and the two youngsters walking beside. A boy of about nine, and a girl, some three years older, dressed in a bright-yellow, calico dress. The landscape rolled through brush grass from raw desert toward the river, with juniper and cottonwood, the going easy for the mules.

The trail Dan travelled went south along the Rio Gila River. He followed it while the wagon rolled out of sight. Overhead, clouds thickened again to bring distant thunder. Lightning speared to the desert on the eastern horizon.

Dan stopped to pull on his slicker and eat some noon antelope jerky. He felt moisture press against him, the sky about to open. Two months on the trail and he wished for a roof. He wanted a floor, a chair to sit at a table and a knife and fork to eat a steak, or a big spoon for homemade beef stew washed down with whiskey or beer. He wanted a velvet bed to caress his woman and hold her close to him. Kneeling beside Rowdy studying the trail, he almost heard the prance of dancing girls kicking up their legs and the tinkle of piano keys while men shouted and clapped their approval. He felt the gentle hand of CK on the back of his neck as he touched her silky leg. Life with a woman had made him soft, as it did any man.

Above the noise of thunder, he thought he heard a gunshot.

A staccato of shots cracked across the sky. He lost count of how many. They came, not from the trail he followed, not down by the shore of the Rio Gila River — the shots came from the direction the family wagon had gone.

Dan threw himself into the saddle and urged Rowdy to run. It had been close to two hours since the wagon had rolled by. The outlaws could have easily turned back and attacked. He rode on, rocking in the saddle with the gallop, watching wagonwheel ruts and looking ahead. With a roll of thunder, the sky opened, pouring rain. Clouds blended with smoke from ahead, black wisps boiling up, thin and coiling. A curtain of gray rain blotted the image but the fire soon released smoke, much of it white, rising steam, spreading up and out.

The gunshots had stopped.

Dan saw the burning wagon ahead,

tucked in a hollow surrounded by juniper. The two black mules were down. Some clothing still burned. Pots and furniture and a saddle were spread about. The Pa lay across the edge of the wagon, bleeding from his back. The boy lay on the ground next to the left, rear wagon-wheel. Dan saw no sign of the girl. Three men in slickers rode out of view, one with the Ma in a green, print dress on his horse ahead of him — Monte Steep. Dan had his Colt in hand. He fired at them but missed in the gallop. They rode out beyond the curtain of rain. He fired again and thought he might have hit something. He grimaced when he realized he might hit the woman.

Where was the girl?

His breathing quickened. He was close. His grip on the Colt tightened. He figured the girl was dead too, so he heeled Rowdy off in the direction of the three men who took the woman and galloped out of the hollow. Rain had put out most of the fire, but the wood

24

frame was mostly burned through. As he rode past he heard a small voice.

'Wait. Wait, mister, please.'

Dan reined in. The girl in the yellow, calico dress crawled out from under the wagon, her arms and face soot black. She shivered and shook, her small face twisted with agony and tears.

The outlaws were getting away. And they had the woman now. He'd have to come back for the girl. Dan pulled the reins around and went to heel Rowdy. The buckskin was ready to run.

'Please, mister,' the girl said again. Gagging sounds came from her.

Steam hissed from the wagon. He didn't want to stop. They were close.

She stood in the rain, much of the soot washing away. The yellow dress clung to her spindly body. Her brown-copper hair hung wet and straight to the arch of her back. Her big, green eyes pleaded with him while she stood shivering, her lower lip vibrating.

Dan felt a flash of thought speed

through his head — the ma or the girl?

Steep was too close. With gritted teeth, Dan heeled Rowdy. After all the years, he had actually seen the man. The hammer of Dan's weapon was already cocked. The killer would soon be dead. Dan's horse squealed as it jerked around again, digging in its hind hoofs to run. Dan intended to shoot Tom Baily in the back, then Levant as he rode after them and to the left. Once beside Steep, he'd shoot him through the temple hoping the woman wouldn't hurt herself falling off. He had never been this close before.

'*Mister*,' the girl cried, sounding desperate.

Dan reined in. Rowdy was confused. The horse turned one way then the other, shook his head, reared back on his hind legs, finally settled and stood. With teeth still clamped tight, Dan swung down from the saddle. They were out of sight now. He holstered the Colt and went to the girl; pulling off his slicker, he slid it around her tiny, skinny shoulders. Tears and rain mixed to wash her face. He held the slicker tight around her and pulled her against him. His heart still pounded in anticipation. There was nothing to her, tall for her age, barely up to his chest, but made up of twigs to look and feel as fragile as she was thin. He was worried he might break some part of her if he held too tight. His thinking was he had to get after the outlaws. He had to get moving.

Dan saw that the father had been shot twice — in the back and the head. The side of the boy's skull had been crushed in. They had taken the wife for sport.

The girl shivered, her face pressed against Dan's chest. 'I hid under the wagon while it burned. Covered myself with sand the best I could. They didn't see me. Pa, Willy — mister, why did they take Ma? They killed our mules; they took our tin box with the copper top. They took Ma. How come they took Ma?'

27

'I have to get after them,' Dan said. 'Now.'

'We go after them together, mister, you and me, got to get them.'

'Come on, then.'

She shook her head. 'We got to bury Pa and Willy.'

'Later. We have to go.'

'We can't leave them in the rain. We got to bury them then go after the killers.'

Dan pushed her away to look at her face, the slicker around her head making her look angelic. Her green eyes held grief and determination. The girl wasn't talking about a quick chase. She wanted the burial — and anything else here — finished before they went after the killers, and stayed after the killers, no matter how long it took.

Dan stared at her. 'What do they call you, girl?'

'My name is Mandy Lee,' she said.

3

With Mandy Lee clinging behind, Dan rode away from the wagon burial site. The shovel with the burnt handle stayed with the skeleton of the wagon. The wagon was too far destroyed for Rowdy to pull. Everything had burned, the charred remains to be left behind. Mandy carried nothing with her. She owned nothing.

Rain had eased to a heavy mist, but mud smeared the trail. One horse rode heavy. Dan figured them moving back to the Rio Gila River. Maybe they'd head for Mexico now. Take the woman and lose themselves in the Yuma Desert south of the border. Have a few sporting days and nights, then leave her body along the trail while they continued east, coming back to rob and kill. Dan didn't have much time, and the girl would slow him down. He wanted all three of them dead in the desert. The girl with nothing had become an obstacle.

Dan reached cottonwoods along the Rio Gila before it became too dark to see clearly. The slender woman's body lay in a tangle of riverbank brush — her face shot half away, her long, green dress ripped to three strips. Mandy erupted in an outburst of shivering tears when she saw her ma. It looked to Dan like the woman had pulled a gun from one of the men and shot herself, rather than go through what the men had planned for her.

After the initial shock and bubbling tears, Mandy used tree branches to dig the grave fifty feet away from the river. Dan wished they had brought the shovel. She worked hard, and Dan helped with the deeper part, using a bigger branch. They wrapped the body in needles and leaves. Dan carried it and gently lay it down. They both used hands and feet to push mud and dirt to cover the body. Dan piled rocks on top and stood back.

Mandy stood sniffling. Dan held his Stetson in front with both hands. He felt he should say some words, but he didn't know what words to say.

The rain had stopped. Clouds kept the night black. The only sound was the gurgle of the river and a swishing breeze that worked along the bank.

Dan said, 'Go well on your journey.'

Mandy said, 'Amen, Ma.'

Dan put on his Stetson.

Mandy shared the one wool blanket, and Dan's saddle-pillow through the night, her head against his chest near his shoulder, his arm around her. She clung to him like small, shivering kindling, and she wept through the hours. He held her, careful of his strength with her fragility.

Sometime during the night, she whispered, 'Who are you, mister?'

'I'm Dan Quint out of Waco, Texas, more recently from Abilene, Kansas.'

'In the morning, we go after those men,' she said. 'We hunt them down

31

and kill them like they killed my family.'

'We'd better find you a horse first,' Dan said.

★ ★ ★

Morning dawned bright and clear with a snap to the air, the space near the campsite dominated by the rocky mound of the grave. Smeared and washed out, the mud left no clear trace of a trail. Dan searched both sides of the river, a mile up and down, another mile inland toward Yuma City. The outlaws were in Mexico and gone. The rain left nothing — no horse leavings, no boot or hoof print, no campground. Not even discarded smokes or thrown food. They had covered their tracks well, and Dan was drawing dry again.

He would start once more, soon as he found a place to leave the girl.

Just before noon, Dan gave up and decided to move on. Rowdy didn't like the extra weight. He'd kicked up a little when Dan, sitting the saddle, swung the girl up behind him.

'Here now,' Dan said. 'Settle yourself.'

Mandy clung tight to Dan, but Rowdy did settle and set off at a walk as Dan eased the reins and gently heeled.

After two hours, Mandy began to twitch behind him.

'Horse hair,' she said, 'chewing up the inside of my legs. I got nothing under this calico.'

Dan reined in. He pulled her off and stepped down. With the blanket behind the saddle, she had a more comfortable ride.

Dan said, 'We'll stop at Gila City, get you a few things, find a ranch or stable for a horse.'

She leaned out to see his face. 'Then where we headed, Dan?'

'You ain't headed nowhere. I'll be finding a farm or ranch for you to stay.'

'No.'

'You got no say, little girl.'

'You must take me with you, Dan.'

'I got to do no such thing.'

'They killed my family.'

'And I'm real sorry about that.'

'I'm going after them.'

'With what? You got no horse, no rigging, no decent travel clothes, no weapon, and no money, none at all. You ain't even wearing shoes.'

'You can buy me that stuff.'

'I ain't your pa. I didn't take you to raise. I found you in the rain, we looked for your ma, and that's the end of it.'

'They can't get away, Dan.'

'They won't.'

'But I got to get them.'

'Nothing for you to get them with.'

She sat behind him in silence for almost a minute. She leaned out again.

'I have money,' she said.

'Where? Pinned to the hem of that yellow, calico dress? That's the only thing you're wearing.'

'In my pa's tin box with the copper top. I got eight thousand dollars in there.'

'Only, you don't have no tin box.'

'They got it, but it's mine. And I got

money in it. Money and a contract that gave my daddy half a silver claim. It's mine now. It's mine, and yours if you help me.'

'Help you what?'

'Get outfitted so we can go after them killers and shoot them down.'

He didn't like talking to her when she sat directly behind him. He didn't want to talk to her at all. She was holding him up. She was making him change his plans.

Moving off the desert, the landscape changed and climbed with ragged foothills. Dan saw a split-log, wooden fence with twenty Texas longhorns milling behind it. The trail became a moist, dirt road. Up ahead he saw a farm with chickens pecking across the yard. As he approached, he saw the farmhouse, a large barn, three corrals — one about twenty feet around, with five horses. A man came out of the barn and shielded his eyes against the sun, watching the buckskin step in. He wore bib overalls and had thin, blond hair around his ears. He watched Dan close.

'Hello the farm,' Dan called.

'I see you,' the man said. His expression showed little friendliness.

Mandy started to slide off Rowdy.

Dan pulled her still. 'Don't step down until asked.'

'Ain't we welcome?'

'We don't know.' He nodded to the farmer. 'Afternoon. A family wagon was attacked yesterday. The girl back there, Mandy, lost everyone. I'm Dan Quint.'

A plump woman came to the door of the farmhouse, wearing a brown, cotton dress, her auburn hair tied up in a bun. She stepped to the big porch and clutched her throat. 'Mercy, a wagon attacked. Invite them to lunch, Meryl. Please.' She waved away flies around the open door and went back inside.

Meryl dipped his head at Dan. 'You heard the missus. Step on down. Help yourself to the well and trough. We got fried chicken and biscuits, and greens from our garden. The school house wagon will be bringing the young'uns from Gila City shortly. We happy to share what we got. Was it Indians? Heard the Apache getting restless.'

'Not this time,' Dan said. 'Outlaw killers.' He clutched Mandy's upper arm and slid her off the buckskin to her bare feet. He swung down behind her and took Meryl's extended hand.

Meryl cocked his head toward Dan. 'Dan Quint. Seems I heard that name before.'

'Common enough,' Dan said.

Meryl stared. 'You from up north, up around Abilene way? A lawman?'

'I worked security there for a spell.'

'You one of Wild Bill Hickok's deputies? I hear he's marshal up there now.'

'No. I never worked for him.'

Meryl rubbed his chin. 'Seems I heard that name someplace — Dan Quint. Well, clean up and come on in.'

During lunch, Dan told the couple about the wagon attack and how the outlaw killers were now riding along the border across Mexico. Mandy remained quiet, but she ate well. Meryl and Ruby had five children aged four to twelve. Their oldest was a girl about Mandy's age. They had old underclothes and a clean dress and shoes that fit. Meryl agreed they might buy one of his Indian ponies that he traded with the Apache for. He didn't have a true Mexican or Texas saddle, but he had an old roping saddle he'd throw in with the sale.

Mandy asked if they had a gun she might buy.

4

The farmer couple had no guns for sale. All they kept on the farm was a double barrel shotgun and an old Sharps .52 rifle. Lately, the Apache had left them alone, but Meryl said that could change at any time. They were close enough to town that one of the children could ride for help, but the thing about Indian attacks was, help always came too late.

It was while Dan, Meryl and Mandy walked to the corral that Meryl snapped his fingers. He hooked his thumbs inside the bib. 'Should have seen it right off — the way you wear your gun. You're the gunfighter, Deadly Dan Quint. It's true, ain't it?'

Mandy spun to stare at Dan, her green eyes shocked and surprised and open too wide for her fragile, triangular face. The faded-pink dress hung from shoulders to ankles. 'Dan?' she said and nothing more.

Meryl did some staring of his own.

Dan nodded. 'None of that means nothing here, Meryl. We just want to buy a horse, so we can ride into town. I got Yankee gold coin or silver coin or paper — whatever suits your fancy.'

'Gold coin,' Meryl said, still staring.

Mandy started to open the corral gate.

Dan put his hand on her arm to stop her. 'Walk around slow outside first. Let them look at you.'

Mandy kept the gate closed. She watched the ponies as she dragged her hand along the top rail of the corral. 'They all look so pretty. Why am I doing this?'

'See which chooses you.'

Five horses watched her intently. Not one looked away. She continued around the corral.

'I think I know the one I want.' She circled back to the gate.

Dan said, 'Go inside, stand at the

gate. Talk low to them. Tell them how beautiful they are.'

She went in. She leaned back against the closed gate and murmured about how pretty they filled the corral and how she wanted one for her own. Her copper-brown hair glistened in the afternoon sunlight.

Meryl stood outside the corral staring at Dan's gun.

An appaloosa dipped his head. The five horses stood in a group away from the gate. A pinto filly held her head high, looking at Mandy. She snorted and took a step forward. She dipped her head and took another step. Mandy kept murmuring. The pinto stepped to her and pressed her head against Mandy's chest. To Dan, Mandy looked tiny and fragile next to the pony.

'She's the one,' Mandy said. She turned to Meryl. 'Does she have a name?'

Meryl grunted. 'Horses is for work. They ain't pets.'

Mandy turned to Dan. 'I'll call her Moccasin.'

When Moccasin was saddled, Mandy mounted the filly for a ride beyond the farm. 'I can't be wearing this dress,' she said. 'Not for what we got to do.' She rode off.

Dan moved next to Meryl. 'How would you like to earn some more gold coin?'

'Doing what?'

'You got five children, a girl the same age as Mandy. She's got nobody, and I can't be taking her with me and what I got to do with them jaspers. Add her to the brood. You'll barely know the difference.'

Meryl shuffled his boots in the barnyard dirt, looking down at them. 'It ain't me, Dan, it's the missus — it's Ruby. When the young'un was born, she says she's done. She don't want no more mouths to feed and take care of. She's about cut me off from hugging and fooling.'

Dan jangled some coins. 'But the girl

42

won't need no taking care of. She's about the age of your oldest.'

'And the oldest is bringing us boy trouble. That's worse than taking care of the youngest. Ruby won't have no part of it.' He shook his head. 'Much as we need the coin, Dan, we just can't do it. Sorry.'

* * *

That afternoon, riding into the town limits of Gila City, Moccasin proved to be obedient and docile. She walked beside Rowdy without fuss. Not that Rowdy did the same. He shook and pranced and kept pulling at the reins.

Dan reined him back. 'Don't be getting frisky now. Hup, whoa, settle yourself.'

'What's wrong with him?' Mandy asked.

'Natural male urges,' Dan said.

'Oh. I grew up around farm animals. I know about male urges.' Mandy twisted in the dress. 'I can't be wearing this. Other people's clothes.'

'You too good for hand-me-downs?'

'My ma made my dresses. My life wasn't riding and hunting killers then. It was farm life and schoolin'. Ma made them pretty, and they fit good, and they were mine.' Her lips pressed tight. The emerald eyes flooded. She turned her head away. 'Sorry.'

Gila City had one main street. Midway along was the marshal's office. Two doors down, a saloon had an upstairs pleasure parlor. Dan wanted strong whiskey to burn his throat. Maybe they had soda pop for the girl. He reined Rowdy in front of the Mid Town Saloon sign and swung down. Mandy did the same.

'We got to get me clothes and a gun,' she said.

'All things happen in their time.'

Through the batwing doors, nine tables with four chairs each, sprawled across a dirty, wooden floor to a hasty-built, plank bar stretched along the length of the room. A tired gent played a tune on an off-key piano about as bad as possible, while a sporting girl giggled, as she was man-handled on the stairs leading up to rooms. Cigarette smoke hung in the air, like a curtain of lace shrouding men trying to out-shout each other. Every table was filled. Two candle-burning chandeliers added more smoke with the light. The bar had men strung like crows on a wire, boot heels caught on the brass rail, overflowing spittoons situated in three places, being spit at, not in. Behind the bar were six liquor shelves and a dirty mirror centered on the wall. The bartender had thin, gray hair and pork-chop face whiskers, his striped shirt sleeves held up by yellow garters.

Dan pushed through to create an empty spot at the end of the bar and asked for a glass of whiskey and orange soda pop. The bartender spent too long looking at Mandy, then turned away and brought the bottles.

Mandy was all eyes, looking around

in wonder. 'You like this?' She had to shout.

Dan tossed down the drink, feeling the sting wash his throat. 'They're not all like this. It's a break from the trail.'

Mandy looked at the doors. 'For a break from the farm, we went to church.'

'That works for some,' Dan said. He turned as a man with a badge came up behind them. Dan already had the loop off the Colt hammer.

'Dan Quint? The marshal wants to see you — in his office.'

Dan remembered Clyde, and said, 'You one of the deputies from the trail, chasing after Steep and his gang?'

He wore a black Stetson low over his eyes. His palm rested on the butt of his revolver in a side holster. 'He says, *now.*'

'Tell Marshal Gene Mount I'll be along when I finish my drink. Or he can come here, and I'll buy him one.'

The palm pushed on the butt. 'The

46

marshal says, in his office now.'

'You keep repeating yourself.' Dan turned his back and put his boot on the rail.

Mandy stood frozen staring at the deputy, the top of her head at Dan's breast bone. Voice noise continued. Only those next to them remained quiet.

One man at the bar said, 'Did he say, Dan Quint?'

Another said, 'Deadly Dan Quint?'

The deputy turned and pushed his way through men, out of the saloon.

'Are we in trouble?' Mandy asked.

'Don't concern yourself. But, we better drink up and go see the marshal.'

'Do you know him?'

'Know of him.'

Mandy shook her head. 'This pop is awful.'

'The whiskey is pretty good. Think I'll finish off another glass.'

'We sleeping outside on the ground again tonight?'

'Maybe I'll take a room at the hotel.

Tomorrow we'll get you outfitted and move on.'

'Good. Don't know when I been so cold.'

'We'll need another wool blanket.'

Mandy slid the pop bottle away across the bar.

Dan lifted the full glass for his last drink.

A big, burly, black-bearded man came up behind him. 'Howdy, stranger.' He stood built like a beer barrel, red and black checked shirt around his girth, wide red suspenders holding up jeans. Bushy hair covered his face, head, and around his neck to his shoulders. A shiny round nose sat below dark, beady bird eyes. 'They call me Bear on account of I'm so petite.'

Dan nodded and polished off his whiskey.

'Lemme buy you another, stranger.'

'Some other time, Bear.'

'I wanna make you a proposition.' He looked at Mandy with such intensity she shriveled and moved closer to Dan.

Dan said, 'We got an appointment with the marshal.'

'Then we can talk another time. Never caught your name.'

'Dan.'

'This can be a moneymaker for you, Dan. I see the little girl is with you.'

'She is.'

'Daughter?'

'I'm taking care of her for now.'

Bear's face brightened with delight. 'Well then, it ain't like she's kin. She ain't kin. Dan, I got a miner's shack sixteen miles outta town, do a little diggin' around for some color. You know, it gets gut lonely out there — especially at night. I'd like to buy that little filly from you. Give you a handsome price for her.'

Dan knew where the conversation was going, and he would not let it get there. 'She's just a girl.'

'Well, I know that. But she can go into training. I can teach her just the way a woman supposed to be. You understand, don't you? She looks bright. She can pick up what to do right away.'

Dan looked into Mandy's emerald eyes. He saw fear there. 'Not tonight, Bear.'

'Well, 'course not, you got the thing with the marshal. Tell you what, Dan, you can go ahead and visit the marshal and leave the girlie with me, you know, so we can get acquainted.'

Mandy nodded at Dan. 'I'm with him.' Her lower lip shivered with fear, as if she realized her life rested in Dan's hands. He controlled what happened to her.

''Course you are, sweetie,' Bear said. 'For now, he's taking care of you. I'm talking about a change in your life. You can be a woman.'

Dan turned to face the big man. 'You ain't listening. Not tonight, Bear. Not tomorrow night. Not any night. Like the girl says, she's with me.'

'Why, that's downright selfish. Let me buy you another drink.'

'We have to be leaving.'

When Dan stepped away from the bar, Bear put his hand on Dan's chest.

'We ain't done talking, Dan.'

'Don't do that.'

'I aim to have me that little girl.'

'She won't even attend your funeral.' Dan used his arm to gently ease Mandy away behind him.

Bear heaved a heavy sigh, beady eyes boring into Dan, lips hidden beneath black whiskers. 'I'll break your back.'

'Not that tonight neither, Bear.'

Since Bear showed no weapon, Dan would not shoot him down — he'd pistol whip him instead.

The batwing doors swung open, and the deputy came back, along with another man wearing a badge. Both men took one look at the crowd's attention and drew their guns.

'That's enough, Bear,' the deputy said.

The other badge had his Remington revolver aimed directly at Dan. 'Keep your hand away from the gun, Dan Quint.'

5

Dan Quint sat at the end of Marshal Gene Mount's desk. Besides the desk, the small office held a two-cell jail, a full rifle cabinet, two more chairs against the wall and a big, front window looking out onto the main dirt road. Dan still had his Colt in the holster.

Marshal Mount looked to be between thirty and forty, dressed in black shirt, pants and boots with a black cartridge belt and holster with the Remington. Could be some men thought black meant authority. He had a square, smooth face, and straight, black hair combed back and down his neck — maybe thought himself another imitation Wild Bill Hickok without the mustache. The black, flat-brimmed Stetson hung on a wall hook.

Mandy sat in one of the wall chairs,

her bare ankles above the shoes, crossed. Deputy Simms had talked Bear down from rage and cut him loose. The marshal sent Simms to fetch Jo.

'Jo?' Dan asked.

'Josephine, my wife. She'll look after the girl while we have our talk.'

The marshal had heavy black eyebrows that joined together when he frowned and talked.

'Dan,' Mandy said from her wall chair. 'I don't wanna go no place with nobody — don't need no looking after.'

The marshal leaned forward, elbows on the desk. 'Now you just never mind, little girl. Jo says there's stuff about you changing she got to talk to you. Things your body is doing you may not know about.'

'My ma told me about them changes. Dan, we got to get going.'

Dan looked down at the rough, wooden floor trying to figure how to angle him and Mandy on down the road.

The door opened and the woman in

Deputy Clyde McCabe's photo stepped in with a smile and a toss of her head. She cut a fine figure in a blue, print dress and her curly, dark hair hanging in ringlets. Big, brown eyes looked across and beyond Dan without interest. The gaze passed over the marshal with equal lack of interest. She turned to Mandy, and the smile widened. 'What is your name, girl?'

'Mandy Lee.'

'Related to the Confederate General?'

'Ma said a distant cousin or something had a connection to the family.' Mandy turned her big, green-eyed gaze to Dan. 'Dan, we got to be moving along.'

Josephine said, 'Let me buy you a hot chocolate at the hotel restaurant, Mandy.'

'No.'

Dan leaned back in his chair. 'Go with her, Mandy. I'll meet you in a bit, and we'll get you outfitted.'

Josephine then looked at Dan with

interest. 'I can do that with her. After our chocolate, I'll take her to the Emporium, and she can pick out what she needs. I'll help with a few dresses.' The smile deepened. 'The cost will be waiting for you, of course. You can meet us there.' She turned to Mandy. 'Come along now, girl.'

The marshal said, 'That's it, then. Dan and me got to talk about how deputies got themselves killed.'

Dan said, 'That suit you, Mandy?'

Mandy nodded. She stood, keeping her gaze on Dan then followed Josephine out the door.

★ ★ ★

The coffee had gone from hot to warm to cold. Dan sat at the end of the marshal's desk knowing he'd had enough and wanted something with more kick, down his throat.

'Where do you think they're headed?' Marshal Gene Mount asked.

'Back along the Mexican side of the

border. The territories are too hot for them now. I reckon they'll come back someplace in Texas, maybe head up to Indian Territory or even the Dakotas.'

'No chance of getting the bank money.'

'Just the reward,' Dan said.

'The black eyebrows thickened together. Just what did Clyde tell you?'

'About them? Or about you?'

The marshal leaned back in his creaking chair. 'Let's start with me, and then swing around.'

'He said you stole the marshal job from him, and the woman.'

'Jo made her choice.'

'I thought that. When you caught the killers, you was going to split the reward.'

'Of course. What's your interest in them outlaws?'

'Personal.'

'You after the reward?'

'I'm after gunning them down, dead.'

'What about the girl?'

56

'They wiped out her family. What do you think?'

'I mean what's *your* intent with the girl?'

'I want her in a safe place.' There were parts of Mandy's tin box, and parts of Monte Steep that Dan figured as none of the marshal's business. Dan didn't care a lot for the marshal. He didn't like the beautiful wife much either.

Marshal Gene Mount said, 'I'm thinking Jo took a liking to the girl. According to the doc, my wife can't have children.' He shrugged. 'One of those things. We might want to take her on as our own. When we heard of her, we talked about it. Naturally, Jo was disgusted with Bear and his offer. That's why she wanted to meet her.'

Dan didn't see that happening at all. He'd take her with him on the trail before he'd let the marshal and his wife influence her. He said, 'That's up to Mandy.'

'She can use more discipline, learn

some manners, get educated. It might be a good life for her.'

'Until you get gunned down on the street.'

The marshal smiled. 'Unlikely that would happen. I can appoint many deputies. I'm popular.'

'So Clyde said.'

'A shame what happened to him.'

'You were supposed to meet him. You and fresh deputies.'

'Yes, we were.' The marshal let it hang there.

Dan sat straight. He'd had enough of the office. He'd had enough of Gila City, and those in it. 'Clyde braced the outlaws alone. It got him killed.'

'He had you, a famous gunfighter, Deadly Dan Quint.'

'I wasn't quick enough, soon enough.'

The marshal sipped cold coffee. 'No, you weren't. I may appoint a few deputies, head on down toward the Texas border.'

'You're a town marshal, not federal.'

'The reward is the same for all.'

'That's right,' Dan said. 'Are we done here, Marshal?' He pushed to his feet, eager to be gone.

'Will you talk to the girl?'

Dan stood at the door. The marshal had not once said her name. 'I'll talk to her. Am I going to be able to get out of town without killing anyone?'

'You mean, Bear?'

'I mean, anyone.'

'You staying at the hotel?'

'Not sure. That's up to Mandy.'

'Tomorrow morning, you tell us what you and the girl decided about her living with us. Jo needs the company, a companion. Somebody to take care of a few chores that need to be done. It will help build the girl's character.'

'Mandy will decide about her own character,' Dan said.

★   ★   ★

Inside the Emporium, Mandy smiled as Dan came in. She looked different. She wore buckskin pants tucked into boots

59

and a yellow, linen shirt with a bright, red bandana around her neck. Her brown-copper hair tied behind her head came out of a brown, short-brimmed Stetson with a neck strap. On a table, she had a heavy, buffalo coat, a yellow slicker, and a canteen.

'Now I can ride,' she said.

Dan said, 'We'll have a scabbard made for the roping saddle. I got a rifle for you.'

Josephine looked neither upset nor pleased. 'I told the proprietor to stay open,' she said, tossing her head for Dan. 'Here is the bill.'

Mandy went to Dan. 'I need one more thing.'

'I know,' Dan said. 'I got it in the saddle-bags, a Colt Navy .36.'

While Josephine held back, Dan and Mandy decided on a belt and a European holster without a flap for Clyde's Colt.

'This holster ain't like yours, Dan?'

'Mine's old — from the war.' He turned so she could see. 'I sliced off the flap and cut a half-moon piece from the holster where it covered the trigger guard.'

Mandy stared with interest. 'I got a lot of learning to do.'

'We'll get started tomorrow.'

After the purchase of two extra blankets, while Mandy looked in the full-length mirror, Josephine pulled Dan aside. 'Gene talked to you about the girl. If she is to come with us, you won't be doing any quick-draw, target-practice tomorrow.'

'That so?'

'Didn't Gene tell you what we wanted?'

'He did.'

'Didn't he tell you to talk with the girl?'

'He did.'

'So, why the gun?'

'Mandy and me done had our talk just now,' Dan said. He had made a decision about Mandy.

6

Dan found a spot in the Tortilla Mountains near the San Pedro River between Gila City and Tucson. His final purchase before leaving town had been a pack mule with vittles and food provisions — dry beans and coffee beans and flour and salt. The buckskin, Rowdy, didn't care for dragging the mule along on a tether. Plus, he had to deal with the attraction of the pinto filly, Moccasin, prancing and teasing beside him. He obviously walked with a life of frustration.

Josephine and the marshal had been left visibly upset.

The campsite nestled under pines and cottonwoods, protected on all sides from icy November winds, the gurgle of the San Pedro flowing by. After tethering the animals, Dan built the campfire high. He and Mandy ate smoked ham and beans washed down with coffee. While the mule stood docile slightly downriver, not so Moccasin and Rowdy, who kicked up rustling and snorting, set to scare fish from the water. After supper clean-up, Dan gulped down two swallows of whiskey. Mandy slid her roping saddle next to Dan's Texas one-cinch.

'The other side of the fire,' Dan said.

'It's too alone over there, and cold.'

Probably a good idea — they could use all three wool blankets plus the body heat. Besides, Dan expected something. He wasn't sure what. 'OK,' he said.

With leaves and the saddle blankets to fit under them and the three blankets to go over, their camp bed was ready. Mandy tucked herself in. Dan piled another log on the fire. He went to the other side and pushed rocks and branches together in a line about his length. He placed his Stetson at the end. He thought about covering it with the third blanket but the night was black under cloud cover. Be hard to see clearly at any distance. On the fire side of the mound, he stretched tree leaves. He and Mandy would need all three blankets.

'What you do that for?' Mandy asked when he crawled under the blankets next to her.

'In case.' He placed the Colt .44 next to his leg.

'Ain't you shedding your boots?' she asked.

'Not tonight. Might need to get up and about in a hurry.'

She snuggled close to him with her thin leg over his, her skinny arm around his neck and her head on his chest. 'You're cozy warm,' she said.

'You could be on a feather bed in a heated room.'

'I know.'

'I can still take you back to Gila City.'

'No, you can't, Dan. You didn't like the marshal and his wife, did you.'

'I did not.'

'She's very pretty.'

'On the outside.'

'How come you don't like them?'

'Part because they never said your name. They didn't look at you as a person. They wanted you to live with them but not as you.'

'I never noticed that.'

'You would have.'

'And?'

'They sucked the life out of my friend, Deputy Clyde McCabe and caused him to get hisself killed.'

'How?'

'Clyde was in love with Josephine and he wanted to be marshal.'

'I don't understand.'

'A few more years on you and you will.'

'Just so you'll be with me then.'

'We'll see.'

'I got nobody else in the world, Dan. My folks is dead. I got no kin I know of.' Her voice broke. 'You're the only person I can depend on. You can toss me to the side of the trail anytime you're a mind to, leave me to all kinds of two-legged buzzards and vermin.'

'Like Bear?'

'Just exactly like that.'

'That ain't gonna happen.'

'I get scared about it. You're all I got. The tin box and you.' She pushed closer to him and sobbed.

He held her close. 'You'll grow and get touched by others. Might not be too good to get next to a loner like me. I got few people myself — a few trail riders, maybe, some ladies in my past.' Dan reckoned to talk about CK in harsh daylight when it wouldn't be part of night wonder.

'We got each other, Dan.'

'You're too young for talk like that.' He didn't want her to get any girlish notions she wasn't grown up enough for.

'No, I ain't,' she said. 'You'll see.'

He had to slip the talk in another direction. If it wasn't for the cold, and what he expected, she'd be on the other side of the campfire. He should have found a room, or a pair of rooms someplace — odd, that he preferred outside and wilderness to inside and towns. Towns had their place at times, especially CK's bed and her softness. With this spindly girl hanging around, he might have inherited a basket of trouble. He already had a woman; he didn't need any girl-child with stars in her eyes and man-fantasy that just wasn't true. He was already thinking about staying in the area. His plan to stick on the killers like a shadow had already begun to change because of the girl. The talk had to get away from her maiden feelings and ideas like it.

'Monte Steep might do something with your tin box. He'll sure spend the eight thousand dollars. What does the box lead to? Can it take us to him?'

Mandy lay still for a minute, her soft hair against his chin. 'How did come you to be there, at our wagon when they was attacking it?'

'I'd been tracking them.'

'You mean since the bank they robbed there in Gila City?'

'Since years before.'

'Why?'

'Steep killed my little brother. Him and the big nose hombre and three other fellas shot me to pieces down in Mexico. I killed the other three. Took months before I could walk.'

'You're after them for revenge.'

'Ain't we both?'

He felt her nod against his chest. 'I wish I could remember all about the tin box. It's tin with a copper top and there's a crown engraved in the copper.'

'You mean like a queen or king?'

'A princess — Pa always called Ma his princess. She went to Europe when she was my age. She saw I got schoolin', readin', writin' and numbers. We left Missouri on account of what was in the box — the papers and the money. Eight thousand dollars in Union cash Pa got from selling the farm and all we had 'cept the Conestoga and the two black mules and some personal stuff. And the contract with his partner, Jeremiah Dickers. The silver claim and Mr Dickers is waiting there for Pa to show.'

'What's that name?'

'Jeremiah Dickers.'

'Waiting where?'

Mandy lay still for a minute. She placed her hand on his right shoulder and held it there. 'Arizona Territory — Pa never said exactly where, what town or mountain or anything. You reckon that outlaw Monte Steep is going to use the tin box?'

'I do, but we got to know where.'

'You think he's headed back now?'

'They might Christmas in Mexico, even wait 'til spring. Or, he may sneak back into El Paso, work his way toward the territories. Too many after him right now, though.'

'What are we going to do?'

'Don't know. Might head north. I ain't going back to Mexico. Let me think on it tonight.'

Mandy snuggled closer. 'You're like a big stove.' She ducked her head under the blankets. 'And you sure smell good.'

Dan kept his head outside, hearing the restless hoof stomp of the horses carousing, above the gurgle of the river. His thinking got serious; serious thinking of Christmas in Abilene.

★ ★ ★

His cheeks were icy cold, but that wasn't what woke him. The shotgun blast lit the coming dawn with a flash and a roar. Rocks on the other side of the dead campfire leaped and scattered over his Stetson.

Dan had the Colt in his hand as he rolled out from under the blankets. Mandy squealed, but he was up and fired a shot at the huge bulk running away between trees. Dan moved after the big, buffalo coat, not enough light to make out features, but he knew who it was.

Bear spun around and fired off his second shotgun blast.

Dan felt rather than saw two tree limbs chip away behind him. He saw the thick, black beard. 'Get rid of it, Bear,' he shouted.

Still running, Bear already had the empties out and another load in. He pulled the second shell from his coat and was shoving it in when Dan fired and missed.

The shotgun slammed shut, and Bear turned around again. 'She's gonna be mine.' He brought the shotgun to his shoulder just as Dan stopped, aimed and shot him in the beard. His hairy head jerked back. The shotgun went off, and Dan felt air whizz close to his left ear. He shot Bear in the forehead, started running toward him as the big man staggered back, then Dan shot him again through the heart.

Bear went down, lifeless as a chopped tree.

7

Abilene, March, 1872 — with Mandy in school and living in a boarding house, Dan had his old security job at the Silver Street Saloon and Pleasure Parlor. Most nights after the saloon closed, he spent upstairs in the suite with CK.

Neither CK nor Mandy was happy to know each other.

Mandy went to school in the mornings with her friends. In the afternoon, Dan rode by, and they headed to the banks of the Smoky Hill River to practice gun work; Mesa, the little filly foal of Moccasin and Rowdy rollicking along. Mandy had already become quick on the draw — she still needed work on accuracy. Dan had put a bullet dent in a fence post about chest high for her practice.

During the following year, Mandy

grew full of confidence. She said, 'I can draw quick as you now, Dan. Come on, stand next to me. I'll bet I'm as fast.'

'Being fast don't mean nothing if you shoot a boot toe, or nip an ear. You won't have time for a second shot. He'll knock you back — he'll flatten you to the ground if he shoots straighter.'

'Just stand next to me,' Mandy said.

'Something else — it could be the fast draw don't mean nothing. Could be the man is on a roof, or hiding behind the corner of a building, or kneeling at a water trough, or if you remember Bear, coming at you with a shotgun in the night.'

'Right next to me, Dan,' she said. 'Come on.' She wiggled and stepped back and forth, her almost-woman face beamed with excitement. She kept her hand next to the holster, ready to draw.

Standing beside the post, Dan hooked his thumb on the hammer of his Colt and squinted at Mandy. She stood taller — the top of her brown-copper hair reached his chin. Her triangle face had lost much of its baby-child softness — her features had sharpened, her skin tawny. She was starting to fill out the denim pants with copper rivet pockets, and the silk blouse. But she carried a restless spirit. She had told Dan they should be on the trail. They weren't going to learn anything stuck in town. Mandy had never killed a man. Dan wasn't sure of her reaction, if or when it ever happened.

And Dan had no intention to draw, If he outdrew her, she might lose confidence. If she came out faster, it was liable to go straight to her head. He slid her off the subject. 'How is school, Mandy?'

'Forget school, Dan. We ought to be down there in Arizona Territory. How we gonna hear anything planted up here — me stuck in school with a bunch of children gawking at how I dress, and you working in some whorehouse?'

'Saloon,' Dan said. 'We're waiting. We

ain't had no word on them.'

'While you're waiting, and drinking too much, you better look closer at CK. She's showing little lines around her eyes. She's got a slump to her walk, getting hefty. She looks tired.'

Dan frowned. That talk was nonsense. CK, who had once been Sweet Candy Kane when she came to town at sixteen — escaped from a Choctaw brave who shot her to leave a scar at the temple in front of her left ear — just before she buried a tomahawk into his head. The tribe had taken her at thirteen after killing her family. Gone from them, she worked as a whore until a customer left her a silver mine in Arizona Territory, which she sold and as Candy Kane, went to Winston-Salem for an education. She now owned The Silver Street Saloon and Pleasure Parlor, and was called, CK — a woman blonde, beautiful and sleek, with devotion to her head of security who shared her upstairs suite.

Dan said, 'She's my woman, Mandy,

and she's barely thirty. And what I'm waiting for is word on any of the gang. That's why I talk to drovers. It doesn't have to be Steep. Any one of them will lead me to him.'

'Sure. I'm just waiting for you to really look at me and come to your senses.'

★　★　★

Dan continued to buy drinks for drovers that came up the Chisholm and moved herds into the railroad stockyards. He asked them about Monte Steep or any member of his gang. In a couple of years, no gunfighters had come to Abilene after the thousand-dollar bounty on Steep. Maybe there was no bounty now that Steep had disappeared. Not so many Texas longhorns came north, either. Sodbuster farmers across the plains bred like rabbits. They plowed the earth, grew hundreds of acres of wheat, and pushed more tribes from the land. Besides

Indian trouble along the plains, grass-hoppers had wiped out the entire wheat crop that year.

Most late afternoons, Dan sat on the saloon porch to sip whiskey and read papers filled with news of corruption and disaster.

Thanks to the rail, Abilene was growing. The most powerful force in the country was the railroads. It wasn't enough for them to acquire cheap right of way for tracks, they took ten to twenty miles on each side of the rails. Since railroad owners were in bed with politicians, no tax was ever required on the land. The owners parceled it for homesteads, and some-times even railroad-run towns.

In June, 1873, Dan Quint received two eagerly anticipated packages in Abilene. One was the new Winchester .44–.40 center fire, fifteen-round, repeating lever action rifle — the '73 Winchester. The other was a Colt .45 single-action, center fire revolver called the Peacemaker. He took to drinking more whiskey while he waited.

Also in 1873, William Cody began the first of his popular Ned Buntline's, The Scouts of the Plains Wild West show. His killing of buffalo gave William Cody the nickname, Buffalo Bill. During one two-day period, he slaughtered close to fifteen hundred buffalo from the side of a train. And trains continued to stop across the plains long enough for shooters to kill off three million buffalo a year. A bill had been introduced to protect the herds, but President Ulysses S. Grant vetoed it.

Newspapers printed two big news events in 1874. A new type of fencing emerged to all but halt Texas longhorn cattle drives across the plains. It was a strand of wire with twisted barbs spaced along it. The wire immediately sold to and strung by sod-buster farmers and ranchers, not in feet or yards, but in miles. Cattle ranchers and wheat farmers spread the word that Texas longhorns carried a parasite dangerous to health. Whether the word was true or not, the price for longhorns fell and eastern meat packers were no long interested in them.

Most significant to Dan Quint, hungry for news of the territories, was the night he met a trail-driving cowhand named Gray Putman.

Sally Green, a petite redhead who earned more in tips than her two-dollar poke fee, was depended on more by CK than other girls. Sally worked as Assistant Manager for extra cash, and ramrodded the saloon and parlor house when CK was busy seeing to the wants and needs of her love, Dan Quint. Dan heard talk among the other girls that when he was away on the trail, Sally Green became closer to CK than Assistant Manager. Even if true, it didn't affect his feelings toward her. She was devoted to him when he was there. No other man touched her close at any time. What she and Sally did while he was gone held no concern for him. She was still his woman.

One spring, Saturday night, a little

after ten, the salon crowded with drovers from a fresh drive, Sally came down the stairs hand-in-hand with a freshly cleaned-up cowboy wearing a trail-tainted, ten-gallon Stetson. Dancing girls kicked up their heels onstage to a lively piano tune, showing all their legs and a little more, to whoops and hollers of trail-end cowboys already through half their whiskey bottles. At the fancy hickory bar, men roared to be heard while homemade cigarette, pipe and cigar smoke waved around the room like dirty, thin blankets. Spittoons were spit at with chewing tobacco juices but seldom hit. Away from the stage, in a corner just inside the batwing doors, Dan and CK sat close, his hand on the inside of her bare left knee, a whiskey bottle and two glasses on the table. Sally brought the cowboy across the room with a smile.

'CK, Dan, this here is Gray Putman,' Sally said, grinning. 'He's fresh off the Chisholm and asked especially to meet Dan.'

CK said, 'After he had a little diversion.'

Sally's cute, thin face brightened in a wide smile. 'Why, of course.'

Dan nodded. 'Set yourself down, Gray.'

Gray wore a green and red checkered flannel shirt under his plain, black cloth vest, and wool pants pushed into his boots. He carried an old Colt Navy .36 low on his right leg, the holster just above the knee. He pulled the tainted Stetson off and held it with both hands over his chest. His head was a mop of sloppy, mahogany hair, fresh-cut and shaved from his neck and around his ears. A boyish face made him look a year or two under twenty. He did not sit. He looked embarrassed by the attention. 'Sir?' he said.

Sally kissed Gray's cheek. 'Maybe see you later, sweetie.' She moved off through the noisy crowd as the piano and dancers finished.

Dan was three-quarters through the bottle. He seemed to get there often lately, going up the stairs to CK's bed, fuzzy-headed with demon drink. 'Wrangler?' he asked Gray when the boy continued to stand.

'Yes, sir. Can we go off someplace, maybe talk alone?'

'Sure we can.' Dan patted CK's leg and swayed, pushing off the chair. He led Gray to the end of the bar, thinking he had to turn his bad habit around, stop drinking so much, get back to what he started. Mandy was right. They had to return to the trail. He was anxious to hear what the drover had to say.

When two filled glasses were in front of them, Gray said, 'I got word, Dan Quint.'

'What about? What can I do for you?'

'You can die for me,' Gray said.

Because of the drink, Dan knew he had little edge. With a tingling forehead and a grip of fear, he didn't see the quick movement as the Navy Colt cleared the holster, wasn't sure of the words. 'What?'

'I got a personal message from Big

Nose Rox Levant. He says, 'Dan Quint has to die.'

Dan spun to the side, clawing for his Colt. The saloon exploded with gunshots as Gray shot Dan across the stomach, then across the chest and through part of his forehead. Three quick shots before Dan cleared his holster. Hammer blows of pounding lead slammed his body. His knees began to buckle. He leaned hard over the bar, but he was slipping. His left elbow hooked on top of the counter then quickly slid off the edge as he sank to his knees and fell back while hot steel burned his stomach, chest and head. A woman screamed. A man on the other side of the room shouted his name. Feet pounded the floor as drunks stomped to the doors. Dan waved to aim, but his vision would not clear. He could not see what to aim at. He felt pain like a saber slice across his chest, another slice pushed blood from his forehead. A flurry of movement circled him as men grabbed the wrangler's gun arm and slammed the boy against the bar.

Dan Quint saw no more because his vision went black.

8

Time passed without notice because Dan Quint was not aware of his surroundings, nor did he see the sky lighten and darken. He clung to his thoughts, felt the present, thought the past — stretched along a grassy edge of the lake on their small family ranch, speaking low secrets with his brother. He lived life with his brother Jordan helping his pa with horses, listening to the soft voice of his ma reading from the good book. Using the old, single-load shotgun, he hunted squirrels with Jordy and Rufus, the wonder squirrel dog, and they splashed in the lake with Rufus barking from the shore — always with Jordy. Time had pushed the killing of blue uniforms at him as he rode, walked and crawled battlefields of the Civil War while lead and steel occasionally slammed into his body. He heard repeated endless talk with Jordy about what they would do once they got home, away from the uniforms, away from the mutilation and blood of war.

Monte Steep and four other deserters had jumped Dan and Jordy when they were riding to Waco to sell the ranch. Their parents, killed by blue belly Yankees, the boys had deserted in 1864, a few months before Lee surrendered, and were off on another life as drovers. Dan took a flintlock ball across his leg before he shot down two of them. A lieutenant in a filthy Confederate uniform fired two shots at Dan, one slug across the right wrist. He'd stepped up to Jordy with a smirk and shot him once in the gut and twice through the chest, then rifled his pockets for gold coins.

Dan killed one more then shot the lieutenant three times, aiming for the head, while the killer jumped and ran for Jordy's horse. One slug grazed his forehead. The killers had wanted horses. Dan got a good look at the killer who, stumbling from his wounds, crawled into the saddle of Jordy's one-eared chestnut and jammed his heels into the sides. The man had one gray eye and one brown eye. Dan kept firing until the gun emptied and Steep rode off, bleeding badly. The others were dead.

Later, Dan's hands were scraped raw from dragging rocks and dirt to cover Jordy's body, knowing but not believing he'd never see his little brother again, loving and missing him. In the first town he reached when going after the odd-eyed deserter-killer, Dan learned the man's name — Monte Steep. Dan had been after him since.

Steep kept sending gunfighters after Dan. Years later, he came himself with four others when Dan tracked the trail to Mexico. They dry-gulched him, chewed up belly skin, grazed his head, and left him to die.

More images passed by as fever burned through Dan. A girl stood in the rain beside a smoldering wagon with her slaughtered family around her, frail, simple calico dress soaked, in tears, calling him back when he was so close to killing those responsible. He continued burning with fever. Pain ate up his belly and chest. His head ached.

Time and events passed by him beyond arm's length while his past life crawled through his thoughts. He watched through a close, dark mesh, unable to see or reach beyond it.

He heard CK say, 'Thank God, the fever's broke, doctor. He's sleeping now.'

The wall of mesh thinned, making him aware of sounds around him.

And he knew he would not the just yet.

* * *

When his thinking cleared, he learned from CK that a month had passed while he recovered in her bed. Mandy Lee visited every day. She kept vigil not only over Dan Quint but across the road from the jailhouse where deputies held Gray Putman. After the shooting, by the time men inside the Silver Street Saloon and Pleasure Parlor got through with him, the shooter had some recovery to do of his own. Being young, and with no broken bones, he healed quickly while he waited for Judge Parker.

A week later, with help, Gray Putman managed to escape the Abilene jail-house.

★ ★ ★

Dan Quint sat in a comfortable armchair of the suite sipping morning coffee while CK told him what had been going on. He wanted Mandy in the room. He missed looking at her.

CK said, 'Mandy will have to tell you what happened.'

'He escaped?' Dan said. 'Where is he now? Who helped him?'

CK sat across from him and held his hand. She was dressed in a pale, pink nightdress, her silky blonde hair down around her shoulders.

Though she looked weary, nothing could take away her beauty. The blue eyes constantly searched his face as if she needed assurance he had recovered. Outside the open window, a wagon rolled by, jangling its hardware. The blacksmith hammered a horseshoe. A horse raced past.

'Mandy is on the way,' CK said. 'I sent Sally to fetch her. Mandy chased after them. She was there. She can say better what happened.'

Just after noon, Dan dozed when the knock came. He still felt weak, but at least he didn't have to be hand-fed soup anymore. CK opened the door then returned to her chair. She had pulled up another for Mandy.

Mandy came in with her Plains Stetson tipped back on her brown-copper hair. She glanced around the room — her emerald green eyes looked at CK in the saloon dress. She bent boldly to Dan and kissed him lightly on the cheek. She sat in the chair next to CK.

Dan immediately saw a change in the girl. Mandy brought in the smell and look of outside. Even with the window open, the room had seemed close with the lack of moving air. She had the trail on her. She had been riding. Sleek and easy moving, she gave a presence of knowledge, knowing where she was and all around her. A change had come to her eyes while she studied Dan's face with an easy trace smile. She still looked so young, so vulnerable, angelic, and yet, something was different.

Dan knew what had happened to her.

CK stood. 'I'll bring lunch.' She kissed Dan on the mouth and left.

Dan and Mandy locked eyes. The change was obvious.

'You're a skeleton,' she said. 'You look weak and fragile. You're not ready for the trail.'

Dan said, 'Who helped the kid escape?'

'One of them what burned our wagon.'

'Big Nose Rox Levant?'

'No, though he was probably close by. From what you told me, it was a small, wiry man, Tom Baily. He got away.'

Dan squinted at her. 'But Gray Putman didn't, did he?'

'No, sir.'

'You drew down on him.'

'Yes, sir. I was watching the jail, looking for a way to stop his thinking and breathing. Tom Baily killed one of the deputies. He had an extra horse, and they lit out in the dark. Moccasin and me and our filly Mesa followed them to their camp about fifteen miles out on the prairie beyond the Smoky Hill River. Before I let them know I was there, I listened in on their talk. Sure enough, Big Nose was gonna be waiting in the Dakotas. They was all three gonna meet to look for gold through the Black Hills. Or maybe steal from them what found it. So, before I stepped into camp, Tom Baily, the coward, jumps his horse and rides out. Gray Putman ain't got nothing but confidence. He done shot down the famous Deadly Dan Quint, killed him dead for all he knew. He ain't gonna have no trouble with a wisp of a girl like me. And he was fast.'

Dan saw it in her eyes. He didn't have to ask. 'What did you do after?'

She leaned forward, eyes dancing with excitement. 'Let me tell you how fast he was, fast on the draw. Let me tell you where I shot him.'

'No, Mandy. I don't care where you shot him. What did you do after? What was the first thing?'

'Nothing. I rode on out, left him there on the prairie. I reckon we got to be heading up to the Dakotas now.'

Dan said, 'You killed your first man. How did it affect you? What did you do?'

Mandy blinked and looked away. 'Nothin'. It was nothin'. I didn't know how fast I was. He was quick, but I beat him easy and shot him dead.'

'And then what?'

'Why you keep asking that, Dan? It was done, and I rode out.'

'You saw his face when your slug tore into him. You watched the pain. He dropped his gun and fell in front of you. The bleeding started. You caused it. You shot and killed the man.'

The emerald eyes filled. 'Stop it, Dan.'

'Mandy, I got to know what you are.'

'I got sick,' she cried. 'I went to my knees and puked my guts up. I couldn't believe I done it. Shooting a fence post is one thing. OK, so I ain't a cold killer like you. It didn't come easy for me.' Her face dropped to her hands while she wept.

'It ain't never easy, Mandy. Unless it's natural in your blood and you get a love for it, it never gets easy. Sometimes it's necessary, but not easy.'

Mandy sniffled. 'I don't want to know if I'm faster than you. When it comes time to shoot down those murdering skunks, I can do it. That's all I know. I can do it if I have to. We got to do it, Dan.'

'Yes, we do,' Dan said.

9

It was the middle of September, 1874, before Mandy Lee and Dan Quint crossed the grasshopper-eaten wheat farmlands of Nebraska to reach the Badlands, and then into the Black Hills of Dakota Territory. Lately, in gun practice with Mandy, Dan noticed that on some draws, his arm tingled and lost feeling which flowed to his thumb. He couldn't cock the Colt hammer. The feeling loss went to his hand, making him drop the weapon. It only happened on occasion and he reckoned it had to do with all the lead slammed through him over the years. The doc had no answer. Dan knew it would clear up before they reached the Dakotas.

Newspaper reports hinted at gold discovery in the Dakota hills. Would-be prospectors rode the rails with their gear into the northern territory then packed south to the Black Hills with pans, shovels, picks and the makings of Long Toms. Others with packed horses came up through the Badlands. Creeks provided flakes for all but no big strikes at first.

Dan and Mandy saw them all around.

The proof of gold provided a fever, filled with dreams and wishes and hope, little ever fulfilled. Every place there was a discovery, Dan saw the camp tents, the overpriced goods and hardware tents, the saloon and one-dollar whore tents. He also observed Lakota and Sioux, sitting their ponies, not yet hostile but watching. The Laramie Treaty had already been violated, the treaty to last as long as water filled lakes and flowed in rivers — white men and their false words once again. Dan knew nothing but trouble lay ahead. After the first feeble effort to keep gold-fever men out, Custer ignored them, and they swept through the hills from pairs to crowds with nothing to stop them.

At the end of September, Dan and Mandy camped close to Rapid Creek along the eastern slope of Black Hills mountain range, not far from Deadwood Gulch where gold had first been discovered. Many tents were pitched along the gulch — it had the makings of a town. Dan moved among them asking about a man with the nose of a saddle horn, maybe with a weasel-looking jasper riding alongside.

Dan rode the chestnut filly, Mesa — the buckskin, Rowdy used as a packhorse, a task he grudgingly accepted with small bucks and snorts each time he was loaded. Mandy was astride Moccasin, her devoted pinto.

On a hot, muggy Tuesday night when Dan returned from his tent rounds, he sat on a rock in front of the campfire and accepted the coffee Mandy handed him. He laced the cup from his whiskey bottle. The pain came mostly from his stomach, and the headaches.

'They're not prospecting,' he said.

'You reckon they gonna rob some-body?'

'They're here to steal and plunder, not somebody but along a path. It's what they do. They come through here a week ago. Not enough gold then. And no Steep.' Dan tilted his Stetson back. 'I can't figure where he is, what he's doing.' He sipped his coffee and rolled the makings for a cigarette.

'Where do we go now?' she asked.

'We head north to the railroad, and keep checking the tent camps. There was a town up there called Edwinton that I think they changed to Bismarck on account of the Northern Pacific Railroad, connects to the Missouri River. I figure if the railroad is bringing these prospectors in, they must be taking some gold out.' When he shifted position, he grimaced in pain.

'You got some bother?' she asked.

'It'll pass. I feel it getting better.'

'Is there anything I can do, Dan? Anything?'

She looked anxious, her hat back,

hair cascading to her shoulders, angel face shiny in the firelight. Men they rode past looked at her the same insolent, hungry way Bear had looked at her, a way Dan didn't like. She may have the image of a woman, but she still thought like a schoolgirl. Her saddle bed spread on the other side of the fire. She wasn't young enough any more, to be lying against him during the night. She seemed to accept that. He granted her to hover over him because he hadn't fully healed. She tolerated the whiskey because of the pain, and he allowed her to take the bottle when she thought he'd had enough.

They continued north, across foothills, through ravines, around granite peaks and down through flat valleys. Considering what Dan heard from prospectors in small tents, he had figured right. The two men had headed for Bismarck and the railroad tracks.

★ ★ ★

Bismarck was hot, dusty and still had tents, but buildings did line the dirt road through town — railroad station, hotel with restaurant, bank, Post Office, Telegraph, hardware, provision stores, three saloons, each with upstairs cubicles to house two-dollar whores, stable and blacksmith. The town marshal's office was next to the railroad station. Tents were set up just outside town to sell mining equipment. The air carried foul garbage smells and the chill of early winter.

Dan concentrated on the saloons and the bank. Mandy got friendly with the restaurant owner and two waitresses. They stayed at the hotel in separate rooms. They ate breakfast and their evening meals together. Dan figured that because of the people they talked to, word would leak out.

Big Nose Rox Levant and Tom Baily visited the town, and they brought friends.

Late Saturday night drunken noise rocked the streets and saloons of downtown. Alone in his room, Dan couldn't sleep. He stretched on his bed, propped against pillows, smoking and sipping whiskey from a glass, thinking of CK, and the girl next door — and how distinct yet similar they were. He heard a light knock on the door and gathered the Peacemaker in his hand.

'It's me,' Mandy said.

Dan crossed to unlock and open the door.

Mandy stepped in wearing a thin purple night dress that showed too much of her for public presence.

'You better cover yourself,' he said.

Mandy frowned. She sat in a worn, green velvet armchair. 'You seen me in less than this. A waitress, Milly, went and got herself wrapped up with one of the gang members.'

Dan returned to the bed, grimaced in pain when he stretched out and lifted his glass to his lips. 'Gang? What gang?'

'They got a gang. Three men. The five of them gonna rob the train, the caboose, a strongbox of gold, supposed to be more'n forty thousand in nuggets.'

'The jasper told Milly that?'

'Bragging on it. Telling her to keep shut — saying, the man, Tom Baily was setting it up. Saying to Milly, him and her gonna leave this hole with his share of the gold — head on down to New Orleans for fun.'

Dan frowned. 'Baily? He ain't got the brains of a fruit-fly. Why not Rox Levant? I'd reckon he'd be in charge, planning and setting it up.'

'Milly says they got a cabin, five miles out. The big nose ain't been around much.' She crossed one leg over the other and swung it back and forth slowly. The night dress parted, but she pulled it together and stopped.

Dan said, 'You'd better go back to your room.'

Mandy sighed. 'Do I look too good to you, Dan? You've seen it all before.'

'You're young and full of mischief and looking for trouble. Go on, out with you. We'll talk over breakfast.'

With a pout, she crossed to the door. He pushed her out and locked the door.

★ ★ ★

In the morning, Mandy was already seated in the restaurant when Dan arrived.

She said, 'I had a talk with Milly.'

Dan sipped coffee. 'And?'

Mandy looked well-rested and sparkling with life. Her smile showed a face fresh-washed and lovely. He didn't know how to accept her — as a girl with woman ideas or a woman with girlish notions. He felt increasing discomfort when alone with her. It had to do with his heart and his own manly notions. Or, maybe the feelings came from old wounds.

She said, 'I told her my man wanted in on the robbery. They could use another gun. I didn't say it was you, just told her to ask her boyfriend what he thought. She did tell me the cabin was northeast of here.'

'About five miles you said.'

She nodded. 'The train pulls out tomorrow, supposed to have the gold in a safe in the caboose.'

'How do they know that?'

'They been watching gold shipments pull out, watching it loaded from the bank.'

Dan rubbed his chin. 'Why the train? Why not hit the bank, get gold and cash?'

'This is a railroad town. Besides town marshals, they got railroad deputies, too many of them around town, he told Milly.'

Milly was not their waitress. After they had ordered ham and eggs, Dan said, 'There's five of them?'

'Four. I forgot. Milly said Big Nose Rox Levant left town. Packed his pony and just rode out yesterday.'

'For where?'

'Maybe to join up with Monte Steep. Milly's man said the territories, down around Santa Fe or Tucson or Yuma.'

Dan stared at her as the breakfast

arrived. 'Are you still committed, Mandy?'

Mandy sat straight, her shoulders stiff. 'How can you ask that? Those coyotes wiped out my family. If you don't kill Tom Baily, I will. I should anyway. He wasn't there shooting your brother, just Monte Steep. Him and the big nose killed my folks and set fire to our wagon. Tom Baily is here, and I'll see him dead.'

Dan remained silent for a spell. He said softly, 'We hit them at the cabin tonight, before they go after the train.'

* * *

The cabin was easy to locate in pines and hemlocks at the end of a hollow, one lantern light from the window, smoke curling from a stone chimney. A half-moon shone enough to cast dim shadows. Dan and Mandy left the horses a quarter mile out, tethered to pines. They split to come in from opposite directions. Dan thought about the Winchester, but they'd be in close quarters. He wasn't even sure the four were all in the cabin. At the corral, he holstered the Peacemaker to climb the rail. He left the rawhide off the hammer. He dropped inside. Five horses stood easy, watching him.

'Quint!' Tom Baily said.

Dan spun to the sound of the voice. Baily had been coming from the outhouse. He clawed at his hog-leg, the cabin lantern light showing eyes wide with surprise. Dan cleared the holster. He felt numbness in his forearm travel quickly to his thumb. He lost feeling in his hand. The .45 Peacemaker dropped onto hay. Baily, with gun in hand, came running for the corral, fired two quick shots, the cracks echoing off canyon walls. Dan dropped and rolled, groping for the .45. Feeling eased back into his hand. By then, Baily was at the corral and had a dead bead on Dan's head. Another shot rang out. Baily's shoulders arched back. The revolver spun from his hand to fall inside the corral.

Another shot tore a silver dollar sized chunk out of Baily's head. He dropped forward into the corral.

The cabin went dark. The door flew open, and three bent figures holding guns exited then split up. Dan was on his knees, the Colt in his hand. He shot the lead man, made him somersault and shot him again once he'd stopped. Dan scooted to a corral post as next to him, hay and dirt were gouged away with a shot. Mandy appeared behind the cabin. She fired twice quickly. A second man jerked. The gun flew from his hand as he splashed into the horse trough.

The fourth man was running for the forest without boots or hat. Dan went over the top corral rail, feeling a stab of stomach and chest pain. He fired a wild shot that chipped bark. The man turned with his arm out and fired. Dan felt the zing as the bullet whizzed past his ear. Mandy fired into the forest behind the man. Dan had him in full sight. Running, he shot the man in the butt, again in the shoulder, missed completely, and shot him once more, through the back of the head. The man stumbled and slammed into a tree, bent double then slid down and lay still.

Mandy ran toward the corral. 'That's it?'

'Four,' Dan said. 'Keep away from the cabin door.'

'You OK?'

'I lost feeling for a spell, but it's all right now.' Dan realized Mandy had saved his life. Without her, he'd have been face down in corral straw bleeding to death. 'Thanks for taking care of Tom Baily.'

Mandy stared at him, still panting. She reached to grab a corral rail while her stomach lurched and her dinner came gushing from her mouth.

Immediately concerned, Dan said, 'You hit?'

Bent with her left hand on the rail she waved her right arm behind her. 'Stay away. I'll be okay in a bit.' Her Plains Stetson hung from its neck strap on her back. She kept her hair away from her face. 'Dan,' she said to the bottom rail. 'I ain't made for this killing stuff. I ain't, I'm telling you, I ain't.'

'We got two more to go,' Dan said.

10

It was the middle of October before Dan and Mandy and their three-horse string crossed from the Badlands, Dakota Territory, traversing the wheat fields of Nebraska and back into Kansas. The land stretched flat; air brought a film of frost during the night. Dan still preferred trail sleeping to towns and hotels. Some days were still warm and muggy.

Once across the border in Kansas, riding side-by-side with Rowdy hauling the pack, Mandy kicked up a fuss. 'I don't know why we got to go back to Abilene. We can find some trail to cut southwest and head for Santa Fe. We got enough supplies. The trail will take us into New Mexico Territory, and we head west to Yuma.'

'I want to see how CK is doing,' Dan said. 'A few days to get there, we'll rest

111

a week then head out to Santa Fe.'

'CK is doing fine,' Mandy said. 'She don't need no checking.'

* * *

Once in northern Kansas, Dan felt sticky and decided to camp along the banks of a river he thought might be the Republican. Jagged hills surrounded them; not a cloud blocked the sun. It was getting close to November, yet the mugginess hung like a shroud during the day. He chose a grassy knoll overlooking the slow-moving water. With camp set and the horses taken care of, he pulled the bag of coffee beans and his ancient hand-grinder and set them by his saddle. His bones ached; not a sharp stab but a dull, constant presence. Mandy ground the beans and got the coffee going. Dan went to the banks of the river and stripped buck-naked then dove in.

'Cold, cold, cold,' he said. The water numbed his wounds in an icy envelope.

He splashed, the water at his waist, and dipped under. He came up to see Mandy on the bank.

She slowly peeled out of her tight, denim jeans and dropped the pink, calico blouse next to her gun belt and Stetson, before she stepped lively into the water. 'Brr,' she said as she pushed through the flow to his side, her brown-copper hair flowing wet behind. She smiled at him and splashed water on his face. She traced her finger along his chest scar. She studied the scar on his belly. 'That looks ugly. It must hurt bad.'

'Sometimes. The whiskey helps.'

'You can't just keep drinking whiskey all day and night.'

'It don't take that much — get up on a buzz, so I don't think so heavy on the pain. When it's healed good, I'll taper off.'

With the water to his shoulders, he eased toward the bank until he was able to lean back on his elbows against the mud. The water felt good now he was used to its cold. She followed and brushed against him, her skin slippery wet and smooth as glass with curves.

'Tell me about the tin box,' he said.

She put her hand on his chest. 'The eight-thousand dollars was in it, and the contract about the silver claim, the partnership.'

'What were your parent's names?'

'Will and Elizabeth. My brother was Willy, nine. Pa had the copper top etched with the crown like that queen across the ocean. He thought Ma was a princess.' She brushed him again.

Dan used his elbows to push farther up the bank. He felt a tingle across his forehead, embarrassed. He felt other changes. She was too close. 'The claim is in the Arizona Territory. Did your pa ever say a town or where it might be near?'

Her face was six inches from him. She shook her head. 'Just Arizona Territory. Dan, quit running from me.'

'I ain't running. You're pushing too

close. What's the name of your pa's partner?'

She frowned. She had to push back and think. 'I don't remember.'

'Think. We'll be looking for him in Yuma.'

Her face brightened. 'I got it. Jeremiah Dickers. I know that's it. Jeremiah Dickers, an older man I seen a couple times — maybe fifty, a lot older than Pa. He said for Pa to bring the eight thousand and they was partners. The claim already proved silver from the mine, and they'd go in fifty-fifty.'

'How did your pa know he was legit?'

'He showed us some silver. And he and Pa worked a mine together when they was younger. Pa knew him.' She brushed him again.

Dan heaved a sigh. 'You better either move away or put something on.'

Mandy frowned. 'What for? It's just you and me in this river. You been seeing me necked in lakes and rivers since I was twelve.'

'You ain't twelve no more.'

She stood out of the water in front of him. 'I filled out some. That makes it good for you, don't it?'

'Maybe you ought to get out and put your clothes on.'

'I know I got no experience, but you can teach me.'

'That ain't gonna happen.'

'You keep running.'

'Not me, you. You're just a girl. Get out of the water and dress like I told you.'

She stuck out her lower lip, but climbed the bank and wrung her hair and started dressing in silence.

Dan climbed out and dressed. He went to his saddle and pulled the whiskey bottle.

* * *

Darkness. Dan sat next to his saddle, one swallow into the second whiskey bottle. He couldn't stop watching her move. He felt urges about her he shouldn't. Not her, his body and what

116

he needed. She put more wood on the fire, the denim too tight. Her saddle was on the other side of the flames where it belonged. She packed the saddle-bags.

'I'll leave out some beans,' she said, 'and the grinder for morning.'

'We can have some of that smoked ham,' he said. His voice was thick — too much whiskey already.

She stepped around the fire and knelt in front of him. 'Are you mad with me, Dan?'

Her face shone in the firelight. Her hair framed her youth, the green eyes, pert nose, clear perfect skin — an angel — the flower of youth — young, a girl, just a girl — young, young, young.

He didn't have the strength. They were together alone too much, and that had to stop. It couldn't continue. He had to end it, somehow. His breathing quickened, became shallow. He wanted to put his hands under his armpits — sit on them — think of something else, the task. He was thinking wrong.

117

His thoughts were dumb.

He reached out and put his hand on the back of her neck and pulled her lips to his. Her mouth opened eagerly. Her body pushed against him. He rolled on top of her and felt her arch against him. He kept rolling until she was on top of him.

He jerked his face away. 'No.'

'Yes,' she said. 'I'm so ready for you.'

'This ain't gonna happen,' he said.

She rose on her elbows to look down at his face, her brown-copper hair hanging to brush his cheeks. 'We gotta get something set between us before it's too late.'

'It's already too late.'

'How long can I keep loving you, Dan, and get nothing back?'

'Girl, you don't know about love. You're too young to know.'

'I know the ache of my need for you, and that I want to be with you always, us together every day and night, and how my body gets so ready for you every time we're together. My ma was married at fifteen. She had me the age I am now. I'm ready. I'm sixteen, be seventeen next week. It's past time for me to start having your young'uns. You got to see that, Dan.'

'I belong to CK.'

'Then why ain't she here on top of you? Why don't she spend days and nights on the trail with you?'

'She has a business to run.'

'I don't hate CK. I admire her. She moved out of the whorehouse, got herself educated and got her own business, and she keeps you happy when you're together. And she's got enough female power to keep you from looking at me with soft eyes. She's got to be a lot of woman to do all that.'

'She's my woman,' Dan said. 'Just her and that's it.'

'It's me on the trail with you. It's me beside you hunting down them killers. You're the one took me outta the rain with my folks shot dead. You're the one who made me love you. You caused it. It's your fault.'

'I didn't mean to. I know you saved my life up there in Bismarck.'

'You got to have me with you, Dan. You got a problem with your arm. You need me, and God knows I need you.'

Dan pushed her aside off him. 'Get over to the other side of the fire, Mandy. That kiss was because I had too much whiskey. It won't happen again, and ain't going no further so don't go wishin' and hopin'.'

She pushed to her knees. 'I'll always wish and hope, Dan. That's about all you leave me. I don't know how long I can keep wishin' and hopin' before I give up.' She shook her head. 'No, I ain't giving up. I got to keep thinking one day you'll come to your senses and know I'm the only girl for you.'

'Don't,' Dan said. 'There's a boy out there for you. He ain't some shot to pieces trail tramp with nothing to give a woman. You need another couple years or so, and you'll find the one for you.'

Mandy stood and went around the fire and stretched out with her head on her saddle. 'I already found him only he's too dumb to know it.' She sniffled and cleared her throat.

'Don't start bawlin',' he said.

'I ain't.' She pulled her blanket up over her head.

Dan stretched out with his own blanket, his Stetson low over his eyes. It wasn't her. She just didn't know any better. He didn't trust himself, his own feelings and urges, and lately, he noticed how good she looked to him. One thing he knew for certain. There would be no more trail riding with the young, beautiful wisp of a girl.

11

In the upstairs suite, Abilene street noise came through the open window. Lying back against the pillow with his usual morning pain, Dan Quint felt CK tight against him, her head on his shoulder.

She pulled blankets up to her shoulders. 'We better close the window. There's a morning chill.'

He kissed her forehead. 'I like the air. We going downstairs for breakfast?'

'Sally will have it sent up. I don't want you out of this bed.'

'I'm headed for Yuma tomorrow.'

'I know.' She hugged him tight.

'Two more to go, if I can find them.'

'Maybe you ought to wait another couple weeks. You're still not completely healed.'

'Nope.' He held her tight. Her perfume filled him. He wanted her.

He'd likely always want her. He thought of the girl in the boarding house and wanted to know what she was doing. He frowned with confusion. 'Tell me what I'm going to do, CK?'

'Leave her with me.'

'She don't need the influence of upstairs. She's liable to take off after me, get herself taken by outlaws or Indians.'

'You can't control a girl in love, Dan.'

'Nothing happened with her, you got to know that.'

She leaned to kiss him wet on the mouth. 'I know. But you like her. Maybe you're falling for her. You keep on and something will happen.'

'So, as a woman, tell me what to do.'

CK went on her elbow, her blonde hair covering the side of her face with the bullet scar on her temple. Her blue eyes searched his face. 'She just turned seventeen, send her to school.'

'What school?'

'A girl's college run by the German-Protestant-Lutheran, Moravian Church

— the Salem Female Academy. I got the brochure. You put her on a train, and you send her to Winston-Salem, North Carolina so she can get herself educated. I wrote them a month ago. I'll front the cost.'

'Don't know when I can pay you back.'

'No need for worry — happy to do it.' She looked down at the bed sheets.

Dan frowned. He tilted her chin up. 'Brochure? How long you had this here brochure?'

She kissed him again. 'Two years.'

A knock came at the door. 'Breakfast,' one of the girls said.

★   ★   ★

Despite her face swollen and wet with tears, Mandy in her full silk dress buttoned to the throat, without a hoop, her brown-copper curls wild around her head and neck, still looked like a pretty girl on a vacation trip. Steam hissed from the train as she stood on the

124

platform, tears flowing. Dan stood in front of her, wishing he didn't have to do what he was doing. CK waited a block away in the buggy.

'She made you do this,' Mandy said. 'I ain't going.'

'Yes, you are. College or boarding school.'

'But we ain't done. We ain't finished.'

'When I find them, I'll write you.'

'You won't. You say you will but you won't. Why are you doing this? How can you do this to me, Dan?'

Dan's guts churned. 'You'll get yourself educated. You'll learn, not be ignorant like me.'

He reached for her, but she stepped back. 'I love you,' she cried. 'I belong to you. We got to be together.'

'That ain't gonna happen, girl. When the hunt is done, I'm gonna marry CK.'

'No, you ain't. You can't.'

'You'll find somebody close to your age. You'll see. It'll work out, and you'll be happy.' He knew he talked more on guess than fact. He didn't like himself, to betray her, to send her away, to make himself smaller in her eyes.

She pressed the soaked handkerchief to her flooding green eyes. 'I'll never be happy. You're killing my insides.'

'All aboard,' the conductor called as he passed. 'Time to get on board, Miss.'

Dan reached to her for a farewell hug. He wanted to hold her.

She pushed him away. 'Don't come near me.' She hiccupped with tears. 'Don't touch me. I hate you for breakin' my heart, for burning my insides to cinders. I hate you for making me dead inside. I ain't never gonna feel nothing again, and I hate you for that.'

Dan shivered, and said, 'You don't mean them words, not hate.'

The train jerked. Mandy picked up her bag and climbed up the steps. 'I despise you. You're old, and shot up and nothing. You let her think your thoughts, have her way with you, make you do what she wants. You let her twist you to her way of thinking. I hate you for that. I want you to die, Dan Quint.

You die in the desert all alone with nobody near you. Die with nobody, not one person to mourn you. Not me, I ain't never gonna think about you again.'

The train jerked ahead while she stood with the door open, just inside, back from the entrance.

'Mandy,' he said. He stood stiff. Her words cut into him like .45 slugs. The pain in his chest came from more than old wounds. He couldn't believe her.

She backed away to the open door as the train rolled ahead.

'You made me dead,' she cried before the door closed. 'I hate you, and I want you dead too, as dead all over as I am inside.' She turned away and stumbled out of sight, bent in tears, the handkerchief pushed against her face, as the train rolled on down the tracks.

★ ★ ★

When day turned dark, hours after the train had left with Mandy, the Silver

Street Saloon and Pleasure Parlor was noisy with ranch hands and gamblers and drifters. CK and Dan sat at their table in the corner around from the entrance doors. They had just finished dinner though Dan didn't eat much. He felt the ache of loss, and pain in his chest, not the loss of a lover but of a friend who had shared close events with him, and now hated him. His whiskey glass sat on the table in front of him. He sighed and looked around. He was weary of the look and sound and the foul air of the saloon, tired of men in crowds, drunk and loud. He missed the clean, quiet smell of the trail. He sipped whiskey and stared at the table top, the bite of Mandy's parting words still clawed at him.

CK put her hand on his. 'Don't go tomorrow. Wait a week or two until all your hurt settles.'

'I go tomorrow,' Dan said. 'Ain't no subject for talk.'

'Dan, she didn't mean those words you told me. She's upset. Her world and her girlish plans have been destroyed. In time, she'll get over it. She'll meet someone and want to introduce him to you, proud to be with the man of her choice.'

'She wants them jaspers as bad as me.'

'She'll get over that.'

He tightened his lips and stared at her, his insides empty with loss. CK appeared happier than she had in weeks — months — years. He wanted her happy. Him riding the trail with a young girl couldn't set good with her. But with Mandy gone now, CK seemed too happy to see it.

'They wiped out her family,' he said. 'She ain't gonna get over that.'

CK leaned toward him. 'Do you still think about your brother? Do you remember it as clear as it happened?'

'I do. What she remembers is worse. She was younger. It happened sooner. She saw her family slaughtered and everything burned up. She ain't gonna forget, no more than me.'

'Do you think she should be on the trail with you?'

Dan leaned back and sipped his whiskey. He shook his head. 'No. It wasn't good for her. She'll be better off, soon as she settles down.'

'And she'll tell you how sorry she is for those words.'

'I don't think so,' he said. He gripped the glass tight, already sorry for what he had done.

'Of course she will.'

Dan stared at CK's lovely, happy face. 'I got a feeling I ain't never gonna see Mandy Lee again,' he said.

PART TWO

SHOOTERS

12

Tucson, Arizona Territory, August, 1876, Dan Quint rode shotgun for the Butterfield Stage Line on the four-up run from Yuma to Tucson. He spent his days sitting a hard plank seat, his '73 Winchester rifle in the crook of his arm. With the word Monte Steep might be somewhere in the Yuma area, Dan thought he might hear something. He sat while his muscles ached with the lunge and jerk of the coach, rolling amongst sharp, towering rock pinnacles, buttes and mesas; bouncing over dry rolling roads, along wind and water eroded canyons of sandstone. Summer afternoon winds kicked hot desert sand at him, stinging his face with grit. In spring, what little rain came, came quick and heavy and flooded the road or swelled rivers and creeks over their banks. In winter, freezing wind blew through the same path as the hot summer blasts, causing him to hunch into his buffalo coat for a hint of warmth. Nights were spent on wayside station rope bunks, or camping the trail.

While he worked, Dan watched Apaches and waited for an answer to his message.

The *Arizona Citizen* newspaper out of Tucson carried his message once a week. Dan wanted to know the whereabouts of Jeremiah Dickers, last known residence, Yuma, Arizona Territory. Dan didn't know if Jeremiah Dickers was in Yuma or not. A reader might recognize the name. The ad showed a hotel contact in Yuma, one in Tombstone, and the newspaper office in Tucson. He had wanted to use his own name but that might have attracted a back shooter from Monte Steep's gang, or another Gray Putnam after bounty — if Steep was still alive — so he just used Box number D-Q.

The way Dan reckoned, Steep had

the tin box with the copper top. He intended to act on it, or already had. Maybe five years had been too long for Jeremiah Dickers to be still involved, but with or without the partner, Steep would have made a move.

There had to be a reason Dan hadn't heard anything about Steep in three years.

Maybe the ad with the name, Jeremiah Dickers, might flush Big Nose Rox Levant out of hiding. Dan would like Levant to come seeking him. He looked forward to that.

The Chiricahua and Mescalero Apache rode their pinto and appaloosa horses restless and mean-spirited. Occasionally, a brave shot the lone rolling stagecoach out of cussed meanness. They weren't killing drivers yet, nor killing, raping or scalping passengers, just putting bullet holes in the stage-top luggage. Dan was always ready when he caught sight of them, and they knew it.

Other southwest Indians — Hopi and

Navajo, acted more peaceable, tending to their small farms. But Dan saw that the cavalry wouldn't leave them alone either. Gold was still scratched for in the Chocolate Mountains north of Yuma, and like the Black Hills up in Dakota Territory, the discovery always seemed to be on Indian land, so Hopi and Navajo also had to be moved to reservations.

Stagecoach passengers were tinhorns, prospectors, ranch owners, gamblers, mountain men, gunfighters — all manner of travelers — and the occasional woman, a school teacher or mailorder-bride. A whore who had saved her money and bought decent clothes, now moving to another town to pass herself off as a grieving widow looking to find a new life, preferably with an established, well-off gentleman. And why not? Everybody had to find a way that worked. Dan still hadn't found his. He still had a quest.

The driver of the four-up was an old, former army scout and stage handler named, Coot Gibbons. He moved through life unwashed, white-whiskered, and cantankerous as his fifty-some years allowed. He carried his whiskey bottle always, and tolerated Dan Quint, barely.

On a warm evening toward the end of August, at an overnight stop out of Pima Village, still two days from Yuma, the four passengers had been fed. The ranch owner, the older well-dressed man who sold buffalo skulls as fertilizer, the travelling salesman, and Coot had bunked down for the night. Only the Indian-fighter remained, sitting on the bunkhouse porch smoking a corn-cob pipe, wearing buffalo hide and buckskin with beads. His white hair hung straight as a flag, warrior-tied and beaded and his white beard all but hid his face.

Dan took his coffee and sat beside the man. He set the cup down and rolled a smoke. 'When you figure the Indians here gonna break out?' he asked. He leaned forward offering his hand. 'Dan Quint.'

The man had a strong grip and piercing blue eyes. 'It ain't like they got no reason — cheated, stolen from, lied to by white-eyes with no sense of honor. I'm called Rapids, on account of my water-rapid white hair and beard. It's the name given me by my Cheyenne squaw. Only she weren't no squaw to me. To me she was female perfection, fluid in motion, willowy, gentle, bright and loving and she treated me as if I was the center of her universe. Me, nothin' but a tracker, too much older than her, no meat on my bones, teeth missing, shot four times, three with arrows — still got a stone arrowhead buried in my side too ornery to pry out.' He shook his white, shaggy head. 'Why would a woman of high quality set so much on a cantankerous, drifting mountain bear who worshipped nothing but her? I tell you no man could have asked for better, or more.' He puffed and squinted. 'Nations up north done

138

broke out, getting slaughtered by the hundreds. Apache are next.' He dragged deep on the pipe and blew smoke. 'Governments ain't nothin' but jaspers — some with character, some without. To the nations, them authority fellas forgot two important life lessons. Ride for the brand. Keep your promises.' He cocked his head to one side. 'Lessee, Dan Quint — seems I recall that name.' He nodded. 'Dan Quint, shotgun rider. Interesting. The name I heard was, Deadly Dan Quint, gunfighter.'

'I've been called that. You talk like your wife parted this earth.'

The blue eyes, set back in sun bronzed wrinkles looked out over the dark desert. 'She has.'

'Sorry to hear it.'

Rapids shook his head. 'Typhoid got her, carried by the white dogs.' His faded eyes continued to look out across the desert. 'Some days, I'm ashamed my skin is white — damned deep ashamed. You get to loving a woman and she's part of you, like your arm — or your breath. You get so used to her beside you, the absence hits you icy cold — makes you shiver sometimes for no reason.'

They sat in silence. Rapids tapped his corn cob empty. Horses snorted from the corral. Heat pressed only slightly less in the darkness than the glare of day. A billion stars were sprinkled through the black night. Dan felt the warmth against his skin. His eyelids were heavy but he felt no call for sleep.

He said, 'Why you taking the stage?'

'Looking,' Rapids said. 'Hunting for a place.' He rubbed a gnarled hand across his lips. 'Rode stages from the Dakotas to Tennessee, out here across New Mexico and Arizona Territories. Might take a look at Californy, move on up to Washington Territory, cross higher, maybe Alaska.' He cleared his throat and coughed.

Dan pushed up to stand on the porch step. 'I can't sleep good inside with all them stars out. I got a pint in my bundle, ain't going to no use. Why don't I bring it on out so we can break the seal?'

'Why don't you just do that, Dan Quint?' the Indian-fighter Rapids said. 'I'll tell you about a fella in Gila City heard about me coming on this here stagecoach, fella says he was told about your newspaper ad there in Tucson, the answer to Box D-Q — says he got something you might wanna hear.'

13

Two weeks later, Dan rode Mesa into the small mining town of Aztec, population 116, about twenty miles southeast of Yuma. In an area of subsistent copper and silver claims, feeder tent towns like Aztec kept miners supplied with needs from coffee beans to whiskey to dollar whores. Dan's Winchester and Colt Peacemaker were cleaned, oiled and fully loaded, as if he expected trouble.

The man Dan looked for was One-Ear Shocky Harris. They were to meet in the twenty by twenty tent with a charcoal-printed plank sign, rope-tied to the front, Saloon. Inside, furniture was crudely constructed from whiskey barrels with more planks stretched across for seats, taller split tree trunks for a bar. About twenty men drank and grumbled inside, dressed miner and dirty.

Dan tied Mesa to the post outside and as soon as he stepped in he heard a shout.

'Quint! Hey Dan Quint! Over here! I'm Shocky Harris.'

One-Ear Shocky Harris wore a bowler and a buffalo coat with rips and had not known a shave or hair trim or bath in a month or more. The missing right ear left a question-mark scar. He shivered and his hands shook.

'Let's get you a whiskey,' Dan said.

'Yeah, let's. I knew it was you on account of you described as a cowboy. You sure-enough punch cattle?'

'I have,' Dan said.

'They said a five-dollar gold piece. The man at the newspaper office said you was paying a five-dollar gold piece.'

'Depends on the information.'

'You brung it? You brung the gold piece?'

Dan nodded to the bartender and held up two fingers. He turned to Shocky. 'And my Colt .45. In case.'

'Ain't gonna be no case. He's here. The man is here in Aztec.'

The bartender's thick, black mustache covered his upper lip. His straight hair was greased and parted down the center of his scalp. Wearing a dirty pink, button shirt with black arm garters, he brought two whiskeys and plopped them on the bar. Dan dropped fifty cents on the hacked-log surface. When One-Ear Shocky Harris gulped the whiskey in two swallows, Dan held up two fingers again. The whiskey came from corn and was cut with something, maybe water, maybe turpentine.

'Leave the bottle,' Dan said.

Shocky nodded with vigor. 'A wise choice.' He held his glass up in a mock toast.

Dan drank his down. 'Is the man here? Jeremiah Dickers?'

'Yeah, Jerry Dickers, got a tent the edge of town. He thinks he's a silver miner but he ain't pulled out enough to feed hisself.' He looked around. 'Surprised he ain't in here. Jerry usually hangs out here at the saloon.'

Dan said, 'Is this the silver claim he was in with Will Lee?'

'Don't know no Will Lee. Jerry, he's kinda a drunk. Just gits enough outta that mine to swallow. Don't do much but drink.'

Dan stared at Shocky's dark eyes. 'What do you do?'

'I got a little copper claim, ain't found much yet.' He squinted at Dan. 'I can see you're wonderin' about the gone ear, how come it to happen.'

'Matter of fact, I wasn't.'

'Apaches jumped me northeast of here along the Pecos, tried to scalp me but I jumped around too much, all they got was the ear. I got away but I couldn't find my ear. I went back and looked and looked but it was gone. I guess the Apache think an ear is good medicine. I reckon they took it. Maybe they prayin' to it or somethin'.'

'So, what's next?'

'Figure I might head up to the Chocolates, try my hand at gold.'

'You'll find a crowd.'

With his second glass empty, Shocky poured shakily from the bottle. 'What do you do, Dan Quint? We all gotta do something, right?'

'I ride stagecoach shotgun.'

Shocky leaned back. 'Get outta here. Sure 'nuff, one of them fancy, velvet and polished wood, four-horse rigs? Ain't you kinda old for that? I hear they got boys doing that job.'

Dan watched Shocky slug down the whiskey. 'Let's go find Jerry.'

Shocky grabbed the bottle. As they pushed through drunken miners and overweight, underdrcsscd whores toward the entrance, Shocky said, 'How come you dress cowhand when you ride stage?'

'Comfortable. Suits me. Which end of town is Jerry?'

'It ain't much of a town. We can walk there in five minutes. Why don't you give me the gold piece soon as we meet him, OK?'

'When I'm ready, Shocky. You going

146

to get tough with me?'

'Hell no, I'm a lover. I ain't even got a gun. I just wanna make sure you got the gold piece for when we meet up with Jerry.'

'I bought the whiskey, didn't I?'

'Come to think on it, you sure 'nuff did.'

Outside the saloon, Dan untied Mesa's reins and led the chestnut as he and One-Ear Shocky Harris walked the dusty dirt road past a series of various sized tents to a small rise. Shocky took a pull from the bottle and shoved it in his buffalo coat pocket with the neck sticking out like a tree branch. The sun hid behind marshmallow clouds as the air turned cool. They climbed the rise to a canvas box tent with a peak roof about ten feet by ten feet.

Outside the flap, Dan said, 'Jeremiah Dickers?'

'Hey, Jerry,' Shocky said. 'Fella here to see you.'

A grumble came from inside the tent. 'Go away,' the voice, said.

Dan opened the flap and stepped in. He saw boxes of many sizes. Empty whiskey bottles littered the dirt and sand floor. One lantern sat on a box, the lens so black it looked impossible that any light would show. The cot was against a wall. The heavy man on the cot wearing a thick brown cloth coat over red longjohn underwear covered himself in a black wool blanket. White hair spilled over a gray-stained, striped pillow. The snowy hair grew down his cheeks and below his chin to his chest. He looked like a destitute Santa Claus. He smelled like an outhouse.

Dan said, 'Are you Jeremiah Dickers?'

One-Ear Shocky said, 'The fella is here to see you, Jerry.'

'Why does he call me Jeremiah? Nobody has called me that in years. I ain't talking to him.'

Dan knelt beside the cot. 'What about your partner?'

'I got no partner.' He remained with his face turned away.

'Jeremiah,' Dan said. 'I wanna talk to you about your silver claim partner, Will Lee, and his eight thousand dollars. You remember, Will Lee?'

Jeremiah Dickers began to turn around on the cot. 'What are you saying?'

Dan said, 'Will was on his way west in a Conestoga, coming with his copy of the partnership papers and eight thousand dollars. He brought his wife, Elizabeth, boy Willy, and his daughter, Mandy. They were gunned down on the trail.'

Jeremiah showed Dan his bushy face, his bloodshot, spiritless eyes. 'Gunned down?'

'All killed 'cept the daughter, Mandy.'

'Where is little Mandy?'

'She ain't little no more. What happened to the claim?'

'A low-life villain swindled me out of it.'

'By the name of Monte Steep, right?'

'No, his name is Zack Deller.'

14

When Dan handed the five-dollar gold piece to One-Ear Shocky Harris, Shocky said he planned three stops. First, he'd buy a bottle of whiskey, then get a decent meal, then visit the whorehouse for a poke. No mention of bath or shave or haircut.

Dan found a ten-dollar mule for Jeremiah, got the man fed, cleaned and shaved, and decently dressed in denim shirt and jeans, and a thick, tan cord coat. Together they rode to Yuma where they got two hotel rooms. Dan ordered more coffee than whiskey and started Jeremiah eating decent meals during the days that followed.

Still, the story of what had happened came in spurts as sporadic as the mind process of Jeremiah Dickers.

Four days before Christmas, in the morning, Dan and Jeremiah sat in the hotel cafe. Wreaths tied with red strips hung on the walls. A bushy fir decorated in ribbons and candles stood close to the corner, reaching almost to the ceiling. Fir needle smells did not overpower what came from the kitchen. The clang of silverware on china plates filled the room over a background of low talk.

'I can't afford endless hotel stays,' Dan said. 'I think you're well enough to stay on the trail.'

Jeremiah Dickers shoveled in his morning ham and eggs. 'Whatever you say, Dan. I don't know what else to tell you.'

'Can you describe Zack Deller?'

'Never met him. Everything was handled through the lawyer and the bookkeeper. They made it slick while they swindled us. Me, I'm still waiting for my partner, Will, after all these years and can't find him, was going to seek another partner. I paid the sixteen-thousand for the claim but had nothing to work it. I needed Will's eight-thousand. I had the original paperwork for the partnership. Four years ago. They stole it all away from me.' He squinted and glanced around the cafe, then shook his head. 'They're watching us.'

Dan cleaned his plate with a buttermilk biscuit then finished his coffee. He frowned. 'Who?'

'Somebody gave One-Ear Shocky more than a five-dollar gold piece. I'm not supposed to be here. I never come to Yuma. That's what they said. The deal with the lawyer what swindled me, Oliver Ashby — it was him, Zack Deller, and Deller's bookkeeper — cute little thing, I think her name was Jenny. I think Ashby, or somebody, told me Deller lay with her sometimes.'

'You remember where the claim is?'

'I think so. I'll draw you a map.'

'Is there a town close by, a place to start? All I know, the claim is northeast of here. Is there a town nearby with records? Is it near Aztec?'

'No. My mind ain't quite straight. I

remember Jenny, but not her last name. I remember the lawyer — Zack Deller's lawyer — Oliver Ashby, Mr Ashby. Me and Will was going through him. I bought the mine for sixteen-thousand dollars from the widow. The widow — ' He shook his head.

'There had to be a town where this happened.'

'There was but I can't remember. It was years ago, so many years. So much has happened.' His bloodshot eyes looked desperate. 'What's gonna happen to me?'

'We'll try to get the claim back. You got a new partner now, Mandy Lee. She'll have the eight-thousand for you.'

'I need some whiskey. Maybe a glass of whiskey will help me remember.'

Dan said, 'No whiskey. We got to get out to the claim.'

'They'll kill us. I'm not supposed to be in Yuma.'

As jumbled as everything appeared, Dan had started putting events and people together. He said, 'Do you know who gave One-Ear Shocky more money?'

'It had to be the gunfighter looking for me. Dan, I'm not supposed to be here.'

'Quit saying that.'

'They told me I'd be dead if I came to Yuma.'

'What for?'

'I still got my copy of the contract between me and Will Lee. I got the original Bill of Sale for the mine claim. Will told me about the tin box, about the paper and money in it. They came up with new paperwork or changed Will's copy if they got his tin box, but I got the originals. I got them hidden, that's the only reason I'm still alive.'

'Where are they hidden?'

'Can't say. Maybe after all these years it don't matter so much. Zack Deller has already pulled hundreds of thousands from the mine.'

Dan said, 'Do you know the gunfighter?'

'Handsome Jack Mills. He ain't no gunfighter — he's a killer. Does killing for Deller. He come through Aztec every week to check on me. When they beat me up them three times, I told them the papers was in another town, somebody else had them. If they killed me, the letter I wrote about the swindle and the papers would be sent to the Pinkertons.'

'Is that so?'

'No.' Dickers leaned forward. 'I got them hidden. I'll tell you where when I can trust you.'

Dan leaned back. It would take too much time to get Dickers' head straight. 'The stage will be in late this afternoon. I got to talk to my boss. Right now, since it's so dangerous for you here, we ride a little out of town where we can set up camp. We'll head for the mine, see how it's operating. You got a lot more to remember, Jerry. But I'll get you out of Yuma.'

Dickers' pudgy face — still red raw with shaving the beard — lit as he sat straight. 'I do remember something. The name of the widow I bought the mine claim from, Mrs Ida Collins.'

'You think she's still around?'

'Oh no, she had an accident after the mine deal was done, got herself killed. Not sure when. I remember something else. Zack Deller married Sarah, Ida's sister. Sarah was a widow too, with two little girls, husband killed in the war like Ida's. She was just a snip of a girl. Deller swept her off her feet, married her, and moved on out to her ranch.'

'Ranch, where?'

'I can't remember,' Jeremiah Dickers said.

* * *

By noon, Dan and Jeremiah Dickers had checked out of the Yuma hotel and were three miles away alongside the stage route. They stopped in a clearing among junipers and Dan gathered mesquite to build a fire under the coffee pot.

Dan said, 'We'll leave the horses saddled. We can hear the stage when it comes along.'

'The stage will be going back to Yuma. I can't go back.'

'I know. I'll talk to my boss. We ride the stage to Tucson on the return.'

'What do we do in the meantime?'

'You remember more. You got paper? I got a pencil.'

'Just a napkin from the hotel cafe.'

'Sit yourself over there and start drawing where the mine is.'

'Not sure I remember clear.'

'Draw it as close as you can. And where you think the ranch might be — and any town.'

Dickers sat close to the campfire where coffee perked.

Dan cocked his head. He thought he heard a noise, the grinding step of sand. A horse? At first he thought it might be the creak and groan of a moving stagecoach out along the road. Then he knew it was something else.

A voice behind him said, 'Turn around slow, Deadly Dan Quint. We gonna find out if you're as fast as they say.'

Lifting the loop from the Colt, Dan took a step to the left as he turned. The afternoon sun was in his eyes. He pulled the front brim of his Stetson lower. He looked at a short, clean-shaven man, under thirty in a black Ten Gallon Stetson. 'You can't be Handsome Jack Mills.'

'The very same.'

'You ain't no bigger'n a minute. The desert wind will blow you away like tumble weed. How come you quick-draw pretenders come so little? That Navy Colt is bigger than you.'

'I'm big enough.'

Dan waited while the short gunslinger stared up at him. 'Well?'

When Handsome Jack's hand touched his Colt grip, Dan already had his Peacemaker in hand and shot him in the forehead, right through the brim of the Ten Gallon Stetson. Handsome Jack's head jerked back and he fell quickly to desert dirt. The Colt flew over his bleeding face.

Another shot rang out. Dan started

to turn toward it when a third shot slammed into him, searing pain through the lower left side of his back. The force caused him to jerk around, bringing his Colt to bear. He bent with his gun arm extended, and saw Jeremiah Dickers throw the paper napkin high, clutch both hands over his bleeding heart, bloodshot eyes wide with disbelief as he fell back against the juniper. The next shot slashed a crease along Dan's left arm just below the shoulder. But he had pinpointed where it came from. He knelt low and with gun arm extended, fired twice. Both slugs tore into Big Nose Rox Levant.

15

Dan pressed his hand against the back wound. 'Ah!' he shouted. Fire tore through his back. He dropped to his knees, Colt still in his hand. The gun began to shake. It fell to the ground. He breathed deeply, picked it up again, and looked where Levant had fallen. 'Why you hombres keep pumping lead through me?'

'If you died like you was supposed to, be no need for so much shooting.' Levant's pistol was too far away for him. Lying face-up, he dug his elbows in the sand trying to move toward it.

Dan pressed against the back wound. He swung his leg out to kick Levant's gun away. 'Shut up while I see if the slug went through.' He groped under his shirt to feel the lower left part of his belly. His hand came away bloody. The slug had pierced through closer to his side than his back. His arm bled more, felt like a branding iron against it, skin chewed and soaking the sleeve of his shirt. Still kneeling, he slid his gun belt up to cover the in and out wound and tightened the buckle. With the Peacemaker back in its holster, he kept his hand pushed against the arm wound.

'You mighta kilt me, Dan Quint,' Levant said.

'I told you to shut up.' Dan pushed to his feet. His head went light. He staggered to Jeremiah Dickers and checked to be sure that he was dead. He picked up the napkin. There was a squiggly line with a Y, maybe for Yuma. A line for a road led to an X to mark where the silver mine was supposed to be. A circle at another corner of the napkin had the word, ranch, printed. A square between them had, *town*. Dan went down to one knee as the napkin became fuzzy. He shoved the paper in a vest pocket and waited, shaking his head.

Big Nose Rox Levant groaned and

shifted, still on his back. 'You got to patch up my leaks, Quint. You caught a lung — I can barely breathe. I think you musta shot my liver.'

Dan staggered to a craggy boulder next to Levant, big enough to lean against. He slid down to sit. His hand still gripped the bleeding arm. The arm bled more but his back still felt on fire. 'You been living a high life, Levant. You put on some tonnage since I last saw you — plump as a hog ready for slaughter.'

Big Nose Levant grimaced in pain, the saddle-horn nose pushed into waddles of cheeky fat, his little eyes like black ants. 'Yeah, had me a chubby *señorita* along the Mexican coast last coupla years, kept feeding me tacos and beans and tequila and her special brand of loving. Pumped me up and wore me out — had to leave her when she got in a family way. Hardly recognize you, old hoss. You're skinny as a pine tree.'

'Where is Monte Steep?'

'Oh, Jesus, I got some pain, Quint!

Oh!' He bit his fat lower lip. He hadn't shaved in a week. 'Steep dumped us. We, his loyal men, stuck with him. Three, four year ago, he just says, 'adios, boys' and cuts loose, leaves us stranded. Heard he changed his name. Even heard he sort-of went legit. Before he left us, he took to wearin' glasses, had a gray shade to the lenses so nobody can see his eye color. Don't know who he is now.'

'I think I do,' Dan said. 'You know where he is?'

'Last I heard a town called Darion, big time citizen, got a thousand-head ranch outside it. I was fixing to go there before you shot me up. He owes me money. Me and Handsome Jack thought Dickers would lead us to him, on account of the old guy left Aztec when I heard he shouldn't. Maybe Monte Steep owed money to Jerry Dickers too.'

'Maybe,' Dan said. His head went light again and he felt his face flush. He pulled the belt buckle tighter. He needed something to wrap his arm.

Big Nose Rox Levant cried out, 'Oh, God! Dan, please, don't let me bleed to death. Patch me up enough so I can make it to a doc.'

'Can't do it, Levant, got to let you bleed on out.'

'What for?'

'On account of what you done.'

'I ain't never done nothing to you. I wasn't even there when Steep shot your brother.' He shifted and groaned some more. 'That was a lotta years ago. OK, I fixed him up good enough to ride and we got outta town, but I had nothing to do with your brother.'

'What about the wagon you torched and the family you killed?'

Levant's fat face wrinkled in a frown. 'What wagon?'

Dan grimaced. 'So many you can't even remember. Down by the Rio Gila River, close to Yuma. Not far from here. You took a tin box.'

'Oh, yeah. But I never shot nobody. It was Monte, he was the one took the tin box and shot the man.'

'Then you killed the boy.'

'I never did no such. The wagon was burning. The boy jumped and misjudged. He come down on the wheel with the side of his head. Split it wide open. Now, you know the boy wasn't shot. Nobody shot the boy. He fell and cracked his head on the edge of the wheel. Wasn't much left of the wagon anyways. Burned up. Wasn't me, Dan.'

'You took the woman.'

Levant coughed with blood in his spit. 'No, sir, that was Monte too. He killed the man and took the woman.'

'You used the woman for sport.'

Levant closed his eyes. 'Okay, yeah. But we only each had one turn. She grabbed Tom Baily's Colt and pushed it under her chin and scrambled her face. Nothing we could do. Guess she didn't want no more of our kinda lovin'. She was such a fine-looking woman, we was gonna take her to Mexico. None of that's got nothing to do with you.' He coughed again with more blood. His eyes closed tight. 'Dan, if you're gonna make me die here, promise to give me a Christian burial. Will you do that for me?'

'No,' Dan said. 'I ain't got strength to bury nobody. You shot it out of me.'

'But, *tell* somebody there are bodies out here.'

'Might be out of it myself in a bit.' Dan looked out toward the road.

Levant wrenched in pain. 'Oh, God, at least say some words over me after I go.'

'There was a witness at the wagon, saw you all, saw what you done. You and Steep both back shot the man, the back and the head. *You* threw the woman on the front of Steep's horse, *you* did.'

'What witness?'

'The little girl saw you. She saw your faces. And that ain't all you done.'

'Not to you, Dan. I ain't crossed you.'

'What about Mexico? You and Monte Steep and three other fellas dry-gulched

166

me those years ago. You killed my horse.'

'Not me, that was Monte. I never wanted to go.'

'But you did. And you back shot the girl's pa, and had sport with her ma, and left them there in the rain with all their belongings burning in the wagon. So, you got to bleed out and die and nobody to think over you again.'

'We don't get help; you'll die too, Dan Quint. And who will think over you?'

'Not me. I ain't gonna die. I'm waiting for a stagecoach.'

★ ★ ★

Dan Quint sat in desert sand leaning against the rough rock, gritty wind blowing, sun hot against him. He slept in a woozy daze, the air turning cold with a setting sun. Lightheaded dizziness came from his loss of blood, or by those other wounds through the years — belly, chest, head, arm, leg. His hand had slipped from his upper arm — the shirt sleeve was soaked. He shook his head to a sound and opened his eyes. Where was his horse Mesa? The chestnut stood tied to a juniper over by the gunfighter's body.

They were all dead; Big Nose Rox Levant, Handsome Jack Mills and Jeremiah Dickers. Mandy would be upset she wasn't there. She wanted to be part of Levant's killing. It was her parents he and Steep had slaughtered. If she hadn't been hiding under that burning wagon, her body would have been added to the family.

The sound came again.

Dan didn't have enough strength to stand. Blood seeped from under the high, tight gun belt. He was losing too much. He rolled against the rock to his right, away from the wounded arm, to his knees. With grunts, he lifted his right knee.

'Hiya!' the stage coach driver shouted from a distance.

Dan used his elbows on top of the

rock to get his left foot under him. Leaning forward he pushed unsteadily while straightening his legs. Sparks of pain shot through his back. When he was standing, he turned around and leaned back. Mesa raised her head, her ears went straight up. She looked at Dan then her head moved as she watched the stagecoach rumble and rattle along the road.

'Hiya!' Coot shouted to the four-team. A kid not twenty rode shotgun. They were coming along quickly, the four-up loping at an easy, noisy gallop.

Dan pushed off the rock and staggered the seven or eight feet to grip Mesa's saddle horn. He untied the reins and draped them over the horn. He didn't have the strength to mount. His leg wouldn't raise high enough for the stirrup. He heard the stage rattle fifty yards away, too far for Coot or the kid to see him tucked in the clearing. With a grip on the saddle horn he turned Mesa's head. He patted her rump and she started to walk toward the road while he stumbled alongside.

The stage was in full view now, coming straight out and moving fast.

'Coot!' Dan shouted. 'Coot!'

Neither heard him. The stagecoach had two passengers, while it bounced and rumbled with so much noise nobody inside heard him. Dan pulled the Peacemaker. He fired a shot in the air, the crack echoed off bluffs under a cloudy sky, pregnant with rain.

The stagecoach kept rolling along.

Dan aimed at the top of the stage where luggage was tied. He aimed toward the front, just behind Coot's head. He fired again. Mesa jerked so hard Dan had to clutch the horn.

The kid stood and turned to look in the direction of the shot, the Winchester to his shoulder.

Coot spun half around, squinted hard, then leaned back pulling the reins tight. 'Whoa!' he shouted. 'Ho, easy.' He stood up from the seat as the horses slowed. He spit tobacco juice over his left shoulder. 'Is that you, Dan?' he said. 'What the hell happened to you?'

* * *

At the coach, the passengers helped — two railroad engineers setting up an office in Yuma. They used clean-laundered shirt strips to wrap the arm and back wounds. Coot hovered outside the stagecoach door. The kid kept the team settled, up front.

Coot nodded to the kid, said, 'This here's Timmy — supposed to be a crack shot but don't look old enough to connect a belt buckle. We'll try to patch you temporary until we get to the doc in Yuma.' He snapped his fingers. 'Dan, I got a wire for you, come in from Abilene two days ago.'

Dan felt lightheaded. 'Coot, I'm about to go out, I'm so woozy. There's dead men out there. Let somebody in town know.'

'Here.' Coot handed the envelope to Dan.

Dan pulled the wire out. The sun dipped below clouds on the horizon, bright red and without warmth, sneaking under the line, barely enough light to see. He had lost feeling in his left arm. The words on the paper were fuzzy but he shook his head until they cleared up some.

Dan.
Come home. Stop. CK is dying.
Stop.
Sally

The words blurred, Dan felt a twist to his heart while the back of his head tingled, flashed then all went black.

16

Dan Quint couldn't travel until the first week of February, 1877. He made stage and rail connections between Yuma and Abilene, passed through desert frost and snow on the plains. He stared at pairs and small shivering bands of pathetic, starving Indians he passed along the way. Aboard the clackety jerk of rail-cars, he stared out train windows, remembering CK, and saw how crowded the territories were becoming.

Dan found nobody to meet him at the Abilene rail station.

He had left his horses and gear in Tucson at the Butterfield stable, close to the Buckley House at the Presidio. Through telegrams with Sally after he started to heal — CK died of influenza and he did not make the funeral. He still had to go because Sally wrote there was paperwork to get through. Otherwise, Dan was finished with Abilene. CK had called it years before. Dan never liked the town. It had no real identity — part of the west, part of the east — little more than a way station, stopping off place for cattle and goods. Dan felt he belonged in the southwest territories, though he still had to have a look at the northwest and Washington Territory. He had only stayed in Abilene because of her.

The loss of CK created a hollow feeling inside his chest, and from time to time he felt a squeeze to his heart. Yes, he had loved her. He loved her the best he could, just not the way she wanted him to. Maybe that wasn't love. Maybe he couldn't love, didn't know how — just wasn't capable.

Finally off trains, he slowly hiked Texas Street to the Silver Street Saloon and Pleasure Parlor in early morning snow, with little street company. He didn't know who the town marshal was and didn't care. Though his wounds had mostly healed, he still felt pain from riding the rocking, railroad passenger cars.

Sally waited in the saloon.

She sat alone at the same table Dan and CK often shared, a pot of coffee and two cups in front of her. The room smelled of stale beer and cold spitting tobacco and puke. The coffee pot sat next to ledgers and papers. The saloon was empty. Upstairs, girls slept after their busy night.

Dan dropped his travelling-bag next to the empty chair. He plopped down hard across from her.

Sally squinted at him, her lips turned down. 'You look worse than when you left.'

'Sorry I didn't make the funeral.'

'Expected. You shoulda made the dying.'

Sally was without make-up. Her small face looked sour with not enough sleep — red hair up but coils of it sprang around her head. She wore a bright-red saloon dress, out of place in the cold morning, low and short to show off her tiny, perky body. Her expression advertised how little regard she had for him. A Franklin stove radiated heat from the end of the bar, another coffee pot perched on it.

Dan sipped coffee. 'Why am I here? You wrote there was business.'

'You don't know how many nights I held her while she cried over you.'

Dan sighed. 'I can wear myself out with regrets, over both CK and Mandy. I can push it 'til I think I got no more reason for living. I ain't going to.'

'Just gonna hit the trail again, right?'

'Right. Get on with your business, so I can get on with mine.'

'CK left the parlor to me.'

'I figured, you was running it.'

'She left the saloon to you.'

Dan sat back with a frown. 'Why?'

'Maybe because she loved you more than life itself, even if you ignored it.'

'I reckon you got good reason not to like me since you shared her bed when I wasn't here.'

'You reckon right, Dan Quint. You not only kill men, you kill hearts. They can call it influenza but CK died of a broken heart. If she hadn't had me, she would have gone sooner.'

Dan sat up straight, grimacing at a twist of back pain. He sipped coffee while he listened to Sally slurp hers. Burning wood crackled from the stove and the soft whisper of falling snow came from outside. 'I got no use for a saloon.'

'I figured that,' Sally said. 'I'm going to buy it from you.' She slid two pairs of paper forms in front of him. 'One is a Deed, the other a Bill of Sale. CK owned the land. Sign all four pages.'

'No. I don't want no money, Sally, you take it all.'

'And have you come back to claim it years down the road? No thanks. I pay you a good price and you walk away, forever.'

Dan shrugged. 'Whatever you say.'

'I'll give you ten thousand dollars. I been running it, along with the parlor upstairs, taking my manager pay and keeping saloon profits for you, three thousand in cash. CK was involved in debt.'

'She owed money?'

Sally's little face twisted in exasperation. 'She made loans to the hardware store owner, the stable owner, and even two gals who started their own tent whorehouse. She bought property out along the Smoky Hill River. She had half-interest in two hotels. That's all collateral I used to get a loan from the bank for your ten thousand. I expect to have it paid back within a year then I'll buy the other half of both hotels. I'm buying the property next door to expand the saloon to include a restaurant, and build the parlor to a Gentleman's Club.'

Dan said, 'If you're not careful, Sally, you'll end up a tired millionaire.'

'I don't give pokes no more, and that's the purpose of it all. I stopped paying for Mandy's college so you got to pick that up.'

'How much?'

'She got two more years — with her room and board, four thousand. I can take care of it and give you six.'

'No,' Dan said as he signed the papers. 'That's ten, plus the three in saloon profit. I want you to send four thousand to pay off the college, then eight-thousand direct to Mandy with a note that it's her daddy's money from the tin box. Give me a thousand; I don't need no more than that.'

Sally frowned. 'Why?'

'When Mandy gets outta college, she's got to pay for half a silver claim. Her Daddy owed it. They'll say it's worth more now, but she only pays eight thousand for her half. And since her partner got himself killed, she gets it all — for the amount her daddy was supposed to put up, what he had in the tin box. She pays it to herself to run the mine since she inherited it all. I still got to prove Jeremiah Dickers was the legal owner.'

'Who's gonna make that happen?'

'I'll make it happen, by pen or by gun, however they want it. I need the address for that there college back in North Carolina. I got to write Mandy a letter about one of the hombres killed her family.'

★ ★ ★

In his Longhorn Hotel room, Dan had stationery on the table with a pencil alongside. He stared at the blank paper and sipped from the whiskey glass, smoking a rolled cigarette. He picked up the pencil and began to write.

Dear Mandy Lee,
Taking pencil in hand on a cold Abilene winter day, I write these words across the land to you. My wish is the words find you well and smart and not hating me so much anymore. My need is to pass on news to you concerning the demise of the late Mr Big Nose Rox Levant, whom I am sure you

remember from killing your family and burning your wagon, and whom I found it necessary to shoot dead along with the late gunfighter Handsome Jack Mills. Sadly the late Mr Jeremiah Dickers caught in the crossfire was also made demised.

I should have writ sooner regarding the shoot-out incident but I was shot some myself and it became necessary to look after my own failing health. I know you wanted to be present at the shooting of the hombres who killed your family and I am sorry you were not able to attend. The money you will soon receive carry reasons that explain themselves. When I am more certain of how the terrain is spread about the silver mine, I will contact you. In the while, now you have grown more, even to being a young lady, I hope the words of hate you spoke to me at our last meeting

have diminished some. *I think of
you often and our days and nights
on the trail and always with
affection. In case my news of the
demised hombres upset you, and
you wish no more contact with
me, I understand. Also, Sally, a
former soiled dove, now rich,
owns the saloon and parlor and
much other property here in
Abilene, as the late CK, once
known as Sweet Candy Kane has
left this earth and is much missed.
Moving pencil from paper, I
remain sincerely*

Dan Quint

17

The middle of June, Dan rode Mesa to Yuma with Rowdy in tow. He boarded the buckskin in the stable to have a horse to ride while he waited for the return trip on the Butterfield. He rode Mesa back to Tucson. Though Rowdy was getting on in years, he still carried Dan on explorations north and northeast of town in search of the mining town of Darion. After each stagecoach run into the Yuma stage station, he took to riding bluffs and hills — searching for evidence of silver mine activity that might lead him to the town.

★ ★ ★

In the heat of July, the stagecoach rumbled and rolled along through the landscape as afternoon wind blew, kicking up dust. Coot drove the four-up. The stage passengers were two young school teachers from New Orleans. The ladies were making a train connection in Yuma to ride across the bridge into California and on to San Francisco where they had teaching positions waiting.

The trip was the greatest adventure of their lives.

Everything excited them — cactus, junipers, blowing tumble-weed, pistols, rifles, the creaking roll of the stage and Apaches on the horizon, sitting their ponies watching. Even an antelope appeared which sent the ladies into a frenzy of admiration. They did appear afraid of Dan though, who reckoned he looked too rough for them.

Five miles out of Gila City, the stage came across a cavalry detachment of nine riders with a young lieutenant in the lead. They rode up to the stage at a gallop, with their rigging and weaponry clanging, kicking up dirt over the sagebrush.

Coot reined in the four-team as the

detachment surrounded the stage. He leaned over toward the stage window. 'You ladies can stretch for a bit.'

Dan set his Winchester on the luggage stacked behind him and swung down from the seat to open the door for the teachers. Once outside, standing on the whipped sand and dirt they looked like fragile white orchids about to wilt. They stepped away enough to show themselves to the cavalry soldiers and the young officer.

The lieutenant reined his sorrel close and watched Dan climb back up to the seat. He touched his hat brim with a smile to the ladies. 'Lieutenant Thompson Crust, at your service, ladies.' He turned the same serious blue eyes to Dan and lowered his voice. Your name, sir?

'Dan Quint.'

The lieutenant nodded, then looked at Coot and got his name. He glanced back at Dan. 'Have we met before?'

'I don't think so.'

The officer's forehead furled. 'Dan

Quint. Aren't you the gunfighter?'

'I've been called that.'

The lieutenant sighed and squinted at the horizon, braced against a gust of gritty wind. 'Have either you gents seen Apaches today?'

Coot said, 'Saw three about a half-hour back — before that, two just before Gila City.'

'What were they doing?'

'Nothing — they sittin' their ponies, watching.'

The lieutenant smiled again at the ladies but talked low to Coot, ignoring Dan. 'A party often hit two miners five miles out of Darion — off work, riding to Yuma for hell-raising. Shot them, tortured them and partially scalped them. We thought they were dead. When we found signs of life we commandeered a wagon and pulled them into Yuma.'

'Are they still alive?' Coot asked.

'That was four days ago. Have no way of knowing. We think the Apache are gathering more braves and weapons

186

to attack the town.'

Dan leaned closer to Coot. 'Where is Darion?'

The lieutenant could not keep from glancing at the ladies, who pranced back and forth along the side of the stage with the open door, shoulders back, their pretty young faces pretending not to care. 'Darion is on the halfway between Yuma and the northern county line, about three miles inland from the Colorado.'

'How many mines around it?' The stage four-team, aware of other horses about, bobbed and pranced in place with snorts. Coot pulled the reins tight. 'Settle down there.'

'It isn't much of a town,' Lieutenant Crust said. 'There are three silver mines close by, the biggest is the Sarah D, named after the owner's wife, I hear.'

'You know who the owner is?'

Coot glared at Dan, as if impatient to be moving along, with no time for damn-fool questions.

'No, I don't. The information I do

have I got from the two men. I doubt they are still with us.'

Dan leaned back. 'Where did you find the wagon to commandeer?'

Coot said to nobody in particular, 'We got to be moving along. We're on a schedule.'

'From a large cattle ranch east of the town,' the lieutenant said.

'Did you get the name of the owner?' Dan asked.

'Of course, the army has to return the wagon.' He gave the ladies another boyish smile. 'The ranch was the Sarah D. The owner's name is, Zack Deller.'

18

Darion, Arizona Territory appeared to be, as the lieutenant said, not much. Dan had already searched north of Yuma but not far enough. Eight miles out, he rode easy letting Rowdy pick his way, met mostly with hot, biting, harsh winds sweeping shallow waves of sand and grit across him. Late afternoon, a pair of Apaches a ways off to the right sat their ponies, jerking with each gust, rifles across saddles, watching him — Dan with his hat pulled low, the bandana tied across his mouth and nose, still feeling the sting of grit blowing across his face, coupled with concern at seeing the stares. Maybe they knew him from rolling stage-coaches.

He rode along the outskirts of Darion, not ready to go in. One main dirt road stretched between five solid, unpainted structures, two buildings a couple stories high. One was a saloon with likely a whorehouse upstairs. The building opposite looked like offices. The third was a general everything store. The fourth had a sign, Darion Hotel. The fifth was a competing saloon, bigger, with more windows upstairs looking out from the whore-house, The Deller Waterhole. That was all he could see from riding slowly around the town. No marshal office within sight. Stretched out beyond were twelve different sized tents. Nobody was outside because of the gritty, blowing wind. The name of the town was block printed on a short cross driven in the ground as if over a grave.

Dan rode on around the outside of the tents and outhouses. Five tents had solid roofs. That was how some towns went. A sturdy wood frame was erected, a square of twenty feet, or ten by twenty, a peaked roof frame on top. Cotton canvas covered everything from roof to ground to give some kind of protection right off. A floor was planked for something solid to stand on and to keep most varmints out. Some places stayed that way until the canvas began to rot and rip. If it looked like the town would be around awhile, more planks were brought in for a roof. The sides could be put up solid with no real rush if the canvas was still good. Wide strips of board were nailed in place to the frame under the cloth.

That made up a town until the source of income — gold, silver, copper, timber — ran out. Then everybody moved on — another ghost town in the making.

Circling Darion, Dan looked for a road leading someplace else. He had come in on a trail from the general direction of Yuma. He saw no railroad tracks anywhere. There had to be a road from the town to the mine, and maybe to the ranch.

Wind continued to blow. Dan had just about decided to enter Darion when off to the northwest he saw a single two-up freight wagon head for the craggy hills. The road led away from Yuma, different to the one he used. Four riders flanked the wagon, each carrying rifles. The wagon was empty.

Dan waited until the wagon was almost out of sight then he eased on to the road behind it. The view was hazy because of wind kicking up dirt and sand. Dan squinted, breathing through his bandana. Four armed men protecting an empty wagon. They came from the direction of Yuma — going where? Going for another load.

After thirty minutes, the wagon and its four riders entered the entrance to silver mine property.

★ ★ ★

In his Tucson room at the Pennington Hotel, Dan practised his draw. The Colt cleared the holster quick, again and again, ready to shoot. His arm and hand felt fine, but he never knew when

192

it might freeze up on him. It had never occurred to him that when he met up with Steep, he might be the one killed. It occurred to him now, though he did not really know where Steep was, and had no Mandy for backup like Bismarck. And, something else he had to realize. His life had taken on a pattern. Killing men had become more important to him than living a life.

★   ★   ★

At the Pennington Hotel a week later, Dan had given notice to Butterfield that he was done riding shotgun. He entered the lobby ready for a bath. Two guests sat in green velvet, sniffed chairs, each reading a paper. The desk clerk, a bald man past sixty with pasty-white skin and spectacles, nodded a greeting.

'Key?' Dan said.

'Letter come for you, sir.'

Dan took his key and turned the letter to sec the return address — Winston-Salem, North Carolina.

★ ★ ★

After the bath and a roasted chicken dinner in the hotel restaurant, Dan rode Mesa west out of Tucson and up the trail leading to hills where pine, firs and spruce grew. He found the creek he liked then dismounted and tied off the chestnut. He gently patted the side of her neck.

'Good girl,' he said. He checked to make sure she had enough rein length to drink.

A breeze whispered through tree needles and brush. The creek, no more than three feet across, gurgled as its flow twisted down to a short waterfall. He sat on pine needles with his back against a skinny tree and rolled a cigarette. When he had the smoke going, he pulled the envelope from his pocket, slid out the letter and unfolded it.

Dearest Dan
You cannot imagine the delight I felt when I received your short

194

letter. What a thrill to hear from my dear old friend way out in the Wild West frontier. I have told my friends of your exploits and of the wonderful time we spent together as you practically raised me, and they are all eager to meet you. They think I am quite the frontier woman, although it has been several years since I rode a western trail.

As you can guess I am fitting in here quite well, and have made many friends, principal among them are my best, best friend from Ireland, Kathleen O'Neal, and, of course my dearest, wonderful Roger Farnsworth. He has just graduated law school and has set up his practice here in Winston-Salem. I help him with forms and depositions and we are quite close.

But you must come to visit! You must tell me in person about what happened and where we are with the villain, Monte Steep. That burning wagon seems so long ago, and so far away. But, I have not forgotten, as I hope you have forgotten the ramblings of a young girl at the train station who knew so little of life those many years ago. She has grown, and moved on, and is quite happy now, thanks to her many friends, and especially to wonderful Roger.

I did receive the money and I understand about it and my participation to get the silver mine. Thank you so very much! It is sad about the demise of CK. I know you cared deeply for her. Sally seems to have taken over nicely. Have you been with her? Are you with her now?

Please contact me when you will come to visit so I may make preparations. Again, it was such a delight to have contact from you! Until I soon see you, I remain affectionately,

Mandy

Dan stared at the page while a breeze wiggled its edges. He read the words again, slower. He searched through sentences looking for Mandy — his Mandy — and found little trace of her. She would be twenty or twenty-one, apparently quite the young lady with new friends and a new life. What a way for him to think. *His* Mandy? Why did he squint when he read the names of her friends? He had no business thinking the way he was. Mandy was her own woman now. He had no connection with her life.

Dan stood and mashed the cigarette under his boot heel. He replaced the letter in the envelope and tucked it away. He'd read it again later, and again, pleased that she'd written. His first reaction was to reject any notion of a visit. Then he realized he really wanted to see her. He had missed her company. He missed *her*. Even now, though he pushed such thoughts away. But he wanted his Mandy, the girl who carried her feelings open and left no doubt who she wanted — the angel, open in her innocence and shameless with her loving emotion. Other men might have taken advantage. He couldn't. He had considered the offering of her love too precious, and undeserving for the likes of him, though she had been a girl too young to know what feeling's meant.

A polished young lady who knew her own mind and had her own friends had written the words he read in the letter, and all she wanted from him was a visit. Why should she want more? The life they had together had been rough and wild and filled with violent killing and hate. No good memories about that. She needed to move on.

Dan stood by the creek looking down the hill. Maybe in spring, he'd take the train cast. The stage shotgun job was done. Why was he dwelling on memories of that spindly young girl anyway?

And who the hell was Roger Farnsworth?

19

Winston-Salem, North Carolina with a population of just fewer than five thousand, built its train station southwest of the town. Tobacco plants pushed toward railroad tracks while the behemoth train screeched and squeaked on in. Dan Quint felt uncomfortable because he didn't like train travel — didn't much care for trains at all — or wagons and coaches. All he needed was a good horse, maybe a pack horse behind. He might cross the country on a good horse.

When the train hissed to a halt, he stepped onto the platform, wearing a dark blue wool suit with new black boots, a silk vest under the coat and a new, gray, broad-brimmed Plains Stetson. The Peacemaker was tucked into a new, black-leather holster below his right hip under the coat. His black hair just covered his neck. His face was clean-shaven except for the half-inch goatee — about as close to civilized as he might get.

The town smelled of growing tobacco and train-boiler coal smoke and steam. Well-dressed men and ladies stood on the platform — some greeted passengers, others looked for greeters. Talk went from squeals of delight to murmurs of affection as folks met each other. Just beyond the station, fancy buggies waited with shiny, fresh-brushed horses standing over equally shiny horse chips.

Dan didn't see anyone who might look like Mandy Lee.

He set the black leather case down. The late morning hung overcast and cool. He felt some humidity, like Kansas in fall, only without the heat. He searched faces on the platform until a girl with bright-red hair held his gaze.

Dan kept the red hair in view. Long and curly, it surrounded a smooth, peach face of about twenty, looking around the platform. She stood with a black man in a white suit. He was shaved bald without a hat. Her deep-blue eyes looked away from Dan then back again. Her expression was quizzical. Not willowy, she looked slightly plumper than full bodied — as if she still had some baby fat, but as she moved it was clear she had blossomed and her bright yellow dress fit her well. Once the blue eyes locked on to Dan, they never left. She stepped toward him with the black man behind her.

'Dan?' she said in a lyrical voice. 'Dan Quint? Sure'n and it has to be you.' She gripped his hand in both hers. 'I dunno, I expected buckskin or a coonskin cap. Sure'n you look, you look . . . '

'Almost civilized?' Dan said.

'Civilized, of course — except around the eyes. I am Kathleen O'Neal. This is Samuel. Take his bag, Samuel.'

Samuel picked up the case and carried it to a four-place open buggy. He put the case on the passenger seat and unlatched the back door.

Kathleen stepped in and pulled Dan to sit next to her. She stared at him as she wrapped her arm around his, her pretty face beaming in a wide grin. She had a trace of freckles across the bridge of her nose. 'You're here, you're actually here.' Her blue eyes danced around every part of his face. 'God, sure'n you're really here.' She hugged his arm tight.

Samuel climbed behind the reins and the black stallion pulled the buggy away from the station.

Kathleen said, 'Mandy has told us so much about you. I feel we are practically intimate.'

Dan raised his brow to her. 'That so?'

Her speech had an Irish lilt to it, the same as a few drovers Dan had met who came to America and out west to make their way. Her voice carried a more pleasant ring. She held his arm tighter. 'Yes, Dan Quint, really. God, you're here next to me. I can feel you. I hardly believe it.'

'How come Mandy ain't here?'

'Oh, she and Roger had a deposition to take. They'll meet us later at the hotel.'

'No school today?'

'It's Wednesday, we only had morning classes. Full schedule tomorrow.' In a breathless voice, she said, 'Did you actually shoot a bear of a man who had a shotgun after he attacked Mandy?'

Dan chuckled. Kathleen O'Neal was cuter than a chipmunk. 'Yes'm. Even his name was Bear.'

'Then it's true. He was going to carry her off to his shack and make her his love slave. Sure'n her stories about you all must be true. And are you living with a whore now?'

'No,' Dan said.

'But you have lived with whores.'

'I have.'

'How wicked.' The buggy pulled to a stop. 'Here we are,' Kathleen said.

Samuel had stopped the buggy in front of a decent-looking establishment, Salem Hotel. Across the street a college campus showed a sign: Salem Female Academy. Two and three-story, white-painted buildings surrounded the college, as well as the hotel. The name change adding Winston must have come after both towns were built. He wondered why.

★　★　★

The reception was at five in the afternoon, peach punch and little, crustless sandwiches, snacks and slivers of white cake with pink frosting served by black waiters. The hall was the size of a mining-town saloon with walls painted a pale green — three, room-long, fluffy white tables, and two candle-chandeliers hanging from the ceiling. Dan had cleaned up while Kathleen returned to her college dorm to change. He now waited in his same suit while girls fluttered in like bright butterflies around a candle flame, most barely beyond their twentieth year, looking and smelling good, chattering to him, introducing themselves with stares of wonder — and names he immediately forgot. They seemed to get some thrill out of touching him as they repeated events in his life for him to confirm. Mandy had told them just about everything.

Dan understood that a small dinner would be at eight with Kathleen and the mysterious Mandy, and with Roger of course.

Kathleen hung on his arm while he mostly verified stories the girls had heard. Her bodice showed more of her than many of the other girls dared. The ladies seemed most shocked by the corral gunfight in Bismarck, where Mandy had shot Tom Baily in the back.

Along about seven, Mandy and Roger arrived.

Mandy appeared popular as the girls flocked to her when she came in. Roger Farnsworth stood tall as Abe Lincoln who he must have admired. He held a stovepipe hat in both hands. He wore the same kind of dark, lawyer suit, and grew a wispy imitation beard. Long and lanky, in his mid-twenties, he had a receding hairline, bony hands and looked at the world over the top of reading spectacles. He ambled, carried himself loose, and obviously worshiped the young lady by his side.

The surprise for Dan was Mandy Lee. He looked for something familiar, a gesture or feature to reveal the spindly, blossoming girl be once knew. Still slender, she had filled slightly more, but not too much. Traces of the girl still showed around her green eyes, a bright emerald shine, but her face had tightened to a good-looking young woman without childhood features. She wore a bright-red dress with tight bodice and waist. Still angelic, she did not look familiar to Dan.

Dan started across the room toward her. She came to him, a path parting, both hands extended, a wide smile but her green eyes expectant, nervous. He intended to sweep her against him and hold her tight. When she reached him, she grabbed his hand in both hers and stopped half-a-step away.

'Dan Quint,' she said with a nervous smile. 'How wonderful to see you again.'

He nodded. 'Mandy.'

Roger slid quickly by her side.

Mandy said, 'Dan, I'd like you to meet my very dear friend, Roger Farnsworth.' She dropped her hands from his. She hugged the lawyer's arm instead.

The young lawyer had a firm grip. 'Much more than friend, I expect. We meet at last, Dan Quint. It would be a waste to say how much I've heard about you. You must know you're admired by every young lady in the room.' Intentional or not, he had excluded himself.

Kathleen hugged Dan's arm as tight as Mandy did Roger's. 'Aren't we a happy quartet? Let's shoo these girls on out of here so we can have dinner.' She kissed Dan on the cheek.

Mandy glared at her with a stone face. 'Don't be so obvious, Kathleen.'

Kathleen frowned. 'What?'

'Honestly, that dress.'

Kathleen stood stiff. 'It doesn't show much more than yours, just more to show. Be nice, Mandy.'

Mandy glanced at Dan, then Roger, then back to Kathleen. 'Of course.' She kept her hug around Roger's arm but smiled at Dan. 'How was the train trip here, Dan?'

Dan ignored the make-words question. He stared at her face with an angry squint that made her wilt slightly. He'd had enough of this shallow banter chatter. He wanted the room empty of giggling girls, colorful and fluttering as they were, only noisy. He and Mandy had serious events to discuss. It didn't look like she wanted them to be alone.

He never should have come.

★　★　★

During a lobster dinner in a private alcove of the hotel restaurant with Riesling wine, Mandy had remained aloof, most of her talk aimed at Roger. It was as if Kathleen and Dan didn't sit at the same table. After dessert, Mandy excused herself and Kathleen to freshen up. Roger Farnsworth asked their permission to fire up a cigar. The ladies reluctantly gave it before they left. The lawyer offered a cigar to Dan, who declined — he wanted to roll his own cigarette. He'd learned J.R. Reynolds had built a factory in town to produce ready-made cigarettes. He still wanted his makings. He reckoned this was neither the time nor place for smoking anything.

After Farnsworth lit his cigar and filled the alcove with smoke, he sipped his Riesling and cleared his throat, acting older than his young years, behaving as a man used to being in charge, or a man who would like to be in charge. 'How long will you be with us, Dan?'

Dan sat back in his chair. 'I leave day after tomorrow.'

His skinny, hawkish face stared, yet

his expression was one of relief. 'That soon? Mandy will be disappointed.'

'I doubt it.'

He cleared his throat. 'I want to thank you for the years you spent raising her.'

'Why? You got nothing to do with them years.'

'Of course. She is quite a remarkable young lady, with a wild, eventful background.'

'Just the way events worked out. What you plan to do with her?'

He blinked with uncertainty. 'Plan? Do? Why, she will be my wife. That should be obvious.' He took a puff on the cigar. 'I understand your concern, Quint. You see yourself as her guardian, as responsible for her personal safety — the father she no longer has.' He leaned forward, his dark eyes slits, as if that expression intimidated others. 'But, perhaps you see yourself as more to her, perhaps you'd like to be more.'

'Perhaps you babble nonsense that ain't none of your business,' Dan said.

Roger sat back. The mood in the alcove had changed. 'I have already drafted paperwork. You have no real claim to her. In three months, she will be of age, and she will need no further connection to you — distant friends, of course. I understand you . . . and a . . . whorehouse madam paid for her education. When we are married, I will see you compensated. Believe me, I can afford it.'

'That so?'

The young lawyer blew smoke toward the ceiling. He rushed on to get everything out as if to make sure Dan fully understood. 'Her future life is here with me, Quint. She will not be giving herself to some horse riding, cattle driving gunslinger out on the western plains with designs on her young mind and body, old enough to know better.'

'That so?'

The young man beamed with confidence now. 'The instant I saw you, I knew what you were after. She has the perfect mind for law. She will be an attorney with her own practice — an office next to mine. That is my plan. That is what I intend to do with her. She will share an office building during the day and my bed during the night.'

'That is if she marries you.'

'It is ordained, Dan Quint.'

'Do your ordaining after I'm gone, lawyer boy. Mandy and me got things to talk about that don't concern you. We got to be alone to do it.'

Roger Farnsworth relaxed with a smug expression. He took a puff from the cigar and sipped his wine with a conceit that showed he commanded the table. 'I know about Monte Steep and the silver claim. She has told me everything — *everything*. I intend for us to take Steep down using the law. If he has swindled her out of her claim, there are legal ways for her to get revenge.'

'*If* he swindled her?' Dan sighed, not liking the news. 'That ain't gonna be enough.'

'The legal way is the only way, Quint.'

'That ain't what I got in mind for Steep.'

'I will not have my fiancée involved in killings.'

'Then there ain't no reason for me to be here. You tell your fiancée that. She don't seem to care much anyway.'

'You still influence her, Quint. I'm trying to wean her from that. Apparently, you are always her hero in a small way, though that has diminished over the last few years. I intend to be her future hero.'

'That so?'

'Yes, that is so. Perhaps you should enjoy yourself with Kathleen tonight. She is apparently smitten with you. She must be desperate with all her pent-up emotions. And you look just frontier enough to bring some wildness to her life.'

'Nothing gonna happen with Kathleen. If I can get myself a ticket, I'll be on a train west tomorrow.'

'That is wise.'

Dan again felt uncomfortable. He

hadn't really belonged since his arrival. And like a few other places he'd visited and wanted to leave, he wished to be away. 'The ladies will be back soon. I got to tell you, Farnsworth. When I come here I didn't know how I felt about Mandy. I wasn't sure the frontier life was for her no more. I see now it ain't. Sure, I thought about her maybe paired with me. It mighta happened once, but it was wrong then. It's wrong now for different reasons. One thing I do know, you ain't the one for her, lawyer boy. There ain't nothing in you to make her happy. I got no way of knowing how close you are to her. If I can, I'll make sure you get no closer, and no intimacy starts or if it started, continues. You get what I'm saying, boy?'

'You're out of your depth, gun-slinger.'

'That so?' Dan Quint said.

20

At midnight, the knock came on Dan's hotel room door. There had been no deep sleep for him, only snatches of dozing while visions of Mandy passed before him. He remembered the campground beside the Republican River in Kansas when she offered herself too young. He remembered the train station and her cruel words of hate to him. She might still feel the same.

When he opened the door, Mandy stood in front of him, wearing the same dress, her emerald eyes searching his face. She had been crying, and that squeezed his heart. He stepped aside silently and let her in. She sat in an armchair, her hands folded tightly on her lap. Her fingers started to quiver.

'You have a chill?' he asked. He pulled one of the blankets from the bed

215

and draped it around her slim shoulders. It was when he touched her shoulders that she became familiar to him. The girl was still in there, his Mandy, his angel.

She stared at her hands. 'Dan,' she said softly.

He knelt in front of her and cupped her small hands with his. 'I have a train ticket for tomorrow afternoon. You'll be safe now.'

'No,' she said. She started to cry. 'You just got here.'

'You have another life now. I ain't welcome. I never shoulda come.'

'You didn't want me, Dan. I ached for you. Years I ached.'

'Mandy, Mandy, you were too young.'

'You've been with teen whores.'

'Not quite that teen.'

'Sally isn't much older. You're with Sally. You've been with her since CK died.'

'Where did you hear that?'

'I . . . just assumed. She has everything now. She'd get you along with the saloon and whorehouse.'

Dan smiled at her. Her face was clean, fresh from a pillow. Now he saw the girl, the features he once knew so well. 'I live in Tucson and Yuma now. I don't even visit Abilene no more. Besides, Sally can't stand me, never could. No, you're wrong, little girl.'

She searched his face again, eyes wet but no more crying. 'You look so old, Dan.'

Dan chuckled. 'I told you that years ago. I got this new dude suit and hat but it's still the same battered, shot-up me underneath. Not sure I ain't still too old for you.'

Mandy smiled. 'Even after all these years, I still miss the trail.'

'Do you, girl? They've been lonesome since you went away.'

'Since you sent me away.'

Dan rose and stepped back and sat on the edge of the bed. 'It's late for you to be out running around. I better get you back to the college.'

'We got a way of sneaking in and out.

Did you do anything with Kathleen?'

'Nothing was ever gonna happen with that filly. I'm only here to see one woman. She ain't much for seeing me.'

Mandy looked back at her hands again. 'So much has changed, Dan.'

'You got yourself a Roger now.'

'Yes. He's been wonderful.'

'He's got plans for you, girl.'

'I know.'

Dan cleared his throat. 'You been with him?'

She jerked her head up to meet his gaze. 'What do you mean?'

Dan felt anxious. He wrung his hands, his breathing shallow, his chest with an ache, not wanting to hear what he might. 'He's a man. You're a woman. I mean nature. You been with him?'

Her hands started to shake. 'How can you say that, Dan? You know I could only be with one man and one man only. But you didn't want me. Maybe you still don't.'

'Maybe things is different now.'

'You told Roger you didn't know. You

said you just knew he wasn't for me. How could you say those things to him?'

'That's the way his trail twisted for me. You ain't the same girl, Mandy, you think different now. Your life has changed. He don't think you want the same end for Monte Steep. He's talking legal stuff. And I ain't even found the jasper yet.'

Mandy sighed. She openly looked over Dan from socks to undershirt to his straight, black hair. Her emerald gaze rested on his face. 'Tell me what happened with Big Nose Rox Levant.'

★ ★ ★

He told her everything since One-Ear Shocky Harris answered his ad in the Tucson paper, *The Arizona Citizen*. About meeting Jeremiah Dickers, learning of the claim and the swindle — learning of a lawyer, Oliver Ashby and the bookkeeper Jenny — the widows who owned the claim, and Zack

219

Deller — Deller marrying the widow, Sarah, moving on her ranch — the shootout with Handsome Jack Mills, Dickers and Levant dying, Yuma, the last known town for Steep, the mining town of Darion. He said he wanted to physically see Zack Deller in order to satisfy his suspicions.

Dan said, 'So what happens when we find Monte Steep, no matter what name he goes by?'

Mandy blinked, an emerald hardness in her eyes. 'We shoot him down like a snake.'

Dan nodded. 'You been practising the draw?'

She lowered her eyes. 'No.'

'Your boy, Roger's got different ideas. He wants to do everything legal.'

'So, we can do it legal. Then we shoot down Steep and anybody riding with him.'

Dan leaned forward and studied that face he wanted beside his. He placed his hand on her cheek. 'You got some wrinkles in your life, girl.'

Mandy sat back in the chair. She pulled the blanket tightly around her. 'I know. The man I admire wants to do things one way. The man I love wants to do them another. I want both.'

'You want both men?'

'That won't work.'

'You might get to liking Roger enough to be with him.'

She shook her brown-copper curls. 'I was jealous the way Kathleen pushed herself on you. That's why I was so snippy. I thought she might have her way.'

'Not with you in the same county, on the same earth.'

Mandy shivered. 'You know you can take me now, Dan, right there in your bed, make me a real woman.'

'Don't think I ain't tempted.'

'Do it. Look at how much I shake? I can't be in the same room with you without wanting you so bad I lose control. Dan, you should have done it on the trail.'

'You ain't ready, Mandy.'

'I couldn't be more ready.' She pushed to her feet and moved to the bed.

Dan stood. He pulled the blanket and let it fall to the floor. He gathered her to his arms and kissed her well, feeling her lips melt against his. Her arms went around his neck and she pushed tight. She continued to shiver in anticipation against him.

Dan slid his hands up to her shoulders and pushed her away at arm's length. 'No.'

Mandy blinked and frowned, breathing heavy. 'Dan, please.'

'We got unfinished business.'

'Yes, right here, right now.'

'You still got Roger.'

'Dan, I've never kissed him like I just kissed you. I never would.'

'He thinks you're gonna marry him.'

'I can't, not if I can have you.'

'You just said you got two men.'

'I only want this with you.'

'I been full of hate so many years — maybe if I was a better man.'

She jumped at him, her arms tight around his neck. 'You're the best man for me.'

'We got to get the business done first, Mandy. And not here. Maybe I'm a dumb jackass for letting this pass but when it does happen, it's forever for me. I got nothing left for nobody else. I got nothing inside me. I don't know how much I can love. Or even if I can.'

'I'll show you. I'll show you how to love. I'll make you want to love. I'll bring more love out of you than you ever thought you had.' She kissed him.

'You know I'm a hard case, Mandy.'

'I can soften your heart. Get me on that train. Take me now and take me with you.'

Dan pushed her and sat her back in the chair. 'I got to find Steep first. It's the only life I lived all these years. I get all soft and sloppy and wrapped in you, what I'll do is get myself killed.'

'But, I'll be with you. I had your back in Bismarck; I'll have it wherever we go.'

'You ain't even been practising. You can't let that skill go fallow.'

'I won't. You'll see. I'll be as fast as I once was.'

Dan knelt in front of her again. Her fingers quivered but she had stopped shaking. He slid his hands along the dress outline of her slender legs. 'I can't have you marrying Roger Farnsworth. That can't happen.'

'Then take me with you.'

'When I find Monte Steep, I'll send you a wire. You come out and we'll go after him together. I don't care about legal parts done and everything right and proper. And I don't want Roger with you. After it's all done, we'll get a good look at each other and see what's what.'

'I can undress now and give you a real good look, see what you remember.'

'You're a lot more woman than the last view I had.'

Mandy heaved a long, shuddering sigh. She closed her eyes. 'You're doing it again, Dan. I got one man I admire and one man I love. You're denying me the man I love. I can't promise you I won't marry Roger Farnsworth. You take that on the train with you tomorrow.'

21

His black hair had grown to his collar, shiny and straight as part of his quarter Cherokee heritage. He left it like that and shaved the goatee to just a long, cookie-duster mustache. He packed his western clothes and pulled on the fancy, dude get-up he'd worn to North Carolina. With a new clothes-look, he'd have to change his name. He decided he'd use his murdered brother's name — call himself J.J. Jordan. He wanted to get entrenched in the town of Darion. He wanted to find the ranch.

* * *

Dan checked into the Darion Hotel, which was rougher and more temporary than many he'd known. With his horses boarded in the stable, he spent time in the Darion Saloon — and found himself back to splintered wood construction, rotgut whiskey, miner brawls, burly bartenders and overweight whores with little charm. The Deller Waterhole across the road looked better, but he wanted to spill drinks with miners, not business owners. In one week, he witnessed two gunfights. Miners were far from home and Darion was no substitute.

The town did have a marshal.

Slipper Hawthorne looked about mid-thirties. In striped shirt sleeves, he carried a belly pot, and kept his thin, straight hair, the color of muddy water, short. He had gray, piercing eyes that swept over Dan as he completed a walk round through the saloon. He wore a pair of Peacemakers and probably had notches on them.

He swung back and stopped in front of Dan, the gray eyes unfriendly with typical lawman suspicion. 'I know you, mister?'

Dan sighed. 'You don't know me, Marshal. The name is Jordan — J.J.

Jordan — I'm here to buy a silver claim. I'm looking for the lawyer, Oliver Ashby.'

'Just had lunch with the gent, he's probably in his office by now, or off in an outhouse someplace.'

'You know him well?'

'Well enough, why?'

'Then you must know Zack Deller.'

'Ain't hardly nobody in town don't know Zack, or of him.'

'I know of him,' Dan said. 'This is his town. You belong to him too?'

The marshal glared. 'If I gotta haul you off to jail, I'm gonna be real mad. I don't like the paperwork.'

'Haul me for what reason?'

'We can come up with something.'

'Don't want no trouble, Marshal. Just looking for a mine.'

'Then you ought to be heading off to the lawyer's office.' He turned and stomped out of the saloon.

Through the batwing doors, Dan saw him cross the road to the fancier Deller Waterhole. One of the regular drunks standing by Dan mentioned that the marshal carried lusty thoughts for the beautiful, fine-figured Sarah Deller — who had come from one of the largest cattle ranches in Kansas just outside Dodge City and was the once-widowed owner with her sister of the Sarah D silver mine. Another drunk mentioned that the fair Sarah was also the wife of Zack Deller, a fact Marshal Slipper Hawthorne had better not forget.

★ ★ ★

With the pot belly stove going and fresh cups of coffee, Oliver Ashby hauled a folder out of a wood file cabinet and spread papers on the oak desk. He frowned at Dan. 'Are you sure about the Sarah D, Mr Jordan?'

They both sat in stuffed, red leather armchairs. Walls were filled with books. The office smelled musty, the stove taking its sweet time bringing warmth.

'I know some of the history,' Dan

said. He had a sip of coffee. It tasted terrible. He put the cup on the desk to remain untouched.

Ashby took a sip of his. He had the shape of a pear, small shoulders wide girth, and his face tapered down to a small, shriveled chin below his pencil mouth. His eyes were brown and revealed nothing about his thoughts. He put the cup down. He leaned back in his chair and made a steeple of his fingers. 'I have to tell you, Mr Jordan. I don't think the claim is for sale.'

'This is the Wild West, everything is for sale — property, towns, people and silver claims. Ain't that true?'

'Well, that particular claim belongs to Deller Enterprises.'

Dan sat straight with a look of surprise. 'Why, don't Zack Deller have an office right there next to yours? I seen it coming in.'

'Yes, he does. Do you know Mr Deller?'

'Only by reputation.'

'You see, Mr Jordan, the mine carries

a rich claim, the vein still thick and pure. Almost a hundred-thousand dollars has been pulled from it.'

'I got a couple million in gold,' Dan said. He thought he should have said more. Why not five million?

It was enough. Oliver Ashby sat straight and put his elbows on the desk. 'Well now, I'm sure we can find a real moneymaker for that amount.'

'Ain't interested in no real moneymaker. I want the Sarah D.'

'Why?'

'Sentimental reasons.'

'I'm afraid Deller Enterprises wouldn't consider selling.'

'Mr Ashby, why don't you put me next to Zack Deller and we'll see what develops. He got a ranch someplace outta town, ain't he?'

'Yes, I'll get in touch with him and we can ride out there in a couple days, if he agrees. First, tell me what is so sentimental about it.'

'How far out is the ranch?'

'About an hour.'

Dan leaned back. 'Didn't the claim used to belong to a coupla civil war widows, Ida, and her sister, Sarah Collins? Sarah had a coupla little girls.'

'It belonged to Sarah's husband, Ben actually. Before he went off to war Ben sold it to her and Ida as partners. That way there'd be no argument about it being handed down to a woman in case he got killed in the war. Courts don't take kindly to women and property. The sisters lived together on the ranch. Because of the war they had no money to operate the mine. The ranch and selling beef to the army barely kept them alive.'

Dan said, 'Then along come this fella, Zack Deller. And he sweet-talked Sarah right outta her heart. Got her to marry him and moved on out to the widow ranch.'

'Yes.'

'Then the sister, Ida, went and got herself killed. Not too clear on how that happened.'

Ashby nodded. 'A horse fall — an

accident — terrible — '

'Was that before or after Zack Deller met the widows?'

Ashby cleared his throat. 'I believe Mr Deller was smitten with Sarah from the first.'

'That's when you met them all and got yourself entwined with their business.'

'Well, the widows couldn't operate the mine and were looking to sell. I arranged for the purchase by Mr Deller. I believe that's when he fell in love with Sarah.'

'Fell in love, sure. Sister Ida got a claw in her gut over that, didn't she? Did she think a swindle was going on?'

'I . . . really don't think so.'

'Too bad about her accident.'

'Yes, terrible. Why are you so interested in the history?'

'Don't wanna buy a pig in a poke. I got to make sure everything was legit down the line.'

'I can assure you, Mr Jordan — '

'You only got a short jump on what

you can assure, mister. Now the way I got it, somebody else was interested in the mine — a coupla fellas from Missouri, one by the name of Jeremiah Dickers, who maybe even paid somebody money for the claim.'

Oliver Ashby shook his head while he blinked. 'Oh no, I'm sure there was nobody else. I would have known.'

'Yup, you sure — 'nuff would have.' Dan crossed his leg and pushed his chair back slightly. Even sitting there, he could pull his Peacemaker and plug the lawyer's lanterns out. Instead, he said, 'Who handled the facts and figures? Wasn't it a bookkeeper? A gal named Jenny . . . Jenny . . . '

'Jenny Troup. Yes, she worked for Mr Deller.'

'How close did she work?'

'A scandal there. They said I was involved. She was married don't you know. When the affair came out, her husband came after me. I'm afraid I had to shoot him.'

'What happened to her?'

'Her husband had kicked her out before he came for me. They had no property. I'm afraid she went down, down, down.'

'Here in Darion?'

'No, last I heard she was in Yuma in one of those . . . places.'

'And the affair wasn't with you.'

'No, of course not. Folks are saying it might have been with some stagecoach shotgun rider on the Tucson-Yuma run. She was sure running with somebody.'

Dan chuckled. 'More likely it was the same office she worked in with that fella, Zack Deller.'

'That's impossible,' Oliver Ashby said, his brow sweating.

22

Two hours after sunrise, Dan was in the saddle. The road to the ranch was farther north than Dan had looked. He kept Mesa almost a quarter mile behind the lawyer. He slowed the chestnut and kept pace out of sight. The barren land rolled to craggy bluffs dotted with sagebrush and mesquite and an occasional juniper. Air carried icy chill making the land look hostile and deadly. No place to be alone or stranded.

Little more than an hour later, the terrain began to change. First, he saw the twisted wire fences with barbs that had popped up across the country. A part of the Colorado River diverted to flow east. A created lake opened irrigation streams in all directions for grass to grow. Longhorns and short-horns roamed along the grass within the fences. The road turned, branched into, and went by a ranch yard. Dan held back.

He wanted to see the man.

He halted Mesa and waited beside the fence. The yard was big enough to swallow Oliver Ashby and his roan. Cattle bawled from every direction. Ashby swung down and went into the house. Dan heeled Mesa forward at a trot. He passed an open gate with an overhead sign, Sarah D, and went on by — a stranger on the trail riding through. He kept the trot until the fence ended and land became cold and barren beside the road once again. He found a juniper just in eyesight of the road and reined up. Some kind of birds had made a fragile nest in the juniper and complained loudly at the invasion. The nest was noisy with occupants who had to be freezing.

Dan could shoot the man as he came by.

He'd have to kill the others — the wife too? The girls? Not likely. The

237

personal rifle guards and Oliver Ashby would open-up on him. And what if his hand froze? Mandy wasn't there. It was enough he knew where the ranch was. He could come back later. There were other things he had to learn. Not now. He wouldn't shoot the man now. But he wanted to see him.

The wait wasn't long.

The birds had settled somewhat. Dan heard the creak of a four-place buggy roll out of the yard. Two rifle-armed riders followed back along each side, their Winchesters aimed at the clouds. Zack Deller drove the buggy with Sarah beside him. The girls sat in back. Zack Deller, the man once known as Monte Steep, who shot down a young lad for his horse and what little gold he had in his pocket, and who slaughtered a family for a tin box and sport with a woman; who dry-gulched Dan Quint down in Mexico, killing his favorite horse.

Other horses coming along made Mesa perk up. Dan patted her neck.

They were fifty yards away from the road, mostly hidden. The buggy came into view. The two girls looked about ten or slightly older. They sat in back, bundled thick with a buffalo hide across their laps, cute faces out of hoods showing red with chill. In front. Sarah sat bundled with mittens wrapped in her own buffalo hide.

Working the reins sat Zack Deller, wearing a buffalo coat, a black, Plains Stetson, gray glasses hiding his eyes. He lightly slapped the reins on the backs of the two black stallions and quickly rolled on by.

Dan felt his hands shiver. A tingle crossed his forehead. It was him — Dan knew it was him.

★　★　★

In Yuma, Dan watched Deller cut his wife loose with the girls on the big general store, as an ore wagon rattled into town from the mine, with two guards riding its flank. Zack Deller then crossed the road to an office door. He stood there watching the wagon. The buffalo coat draped wide on him. His face had puffed over the years yet he remained clean-shaven. He tracked with his gray glasses as the ore wagon passed. The two guards nodded a greeting. Deller looked up and down the street. The gray-lensed glasses passed over Dan sitting Mesa in front of the saloon. There was no pause or recognition. Deller then took off his glasses and wiped them clean with a handkerchief. He again turned to the wagon, his one gray and one brown eye briefly on display. He put the glasses back on and went into the office.

Dan moved Mesa off to follow the ore wagon. The two personal guards lounged outside the office door. They gave him a glance as he rode by. At the railroad station, he watched blacks unload ore rocks onto a rail car. It would be sent to a trammel or rock crusher somewhere in California to separate rock from silver. That operation might be sorted out later.

Dan needed a drink. All those years, on the trail crisscrossing the country in search of a man — the towns, the saloons, the hotels, the camps, the women — and he was here, the search had finally ended. Monte Steep was here. Dan only had to find the whore, Jenny Troup, then he could wire Mandy Lee to come on out. They had their man.

23

The lawyer rode the roan — Dan was on Mesa. They trotted the same road Dan had been on two mornings before on his last visit to the ranch. This time they went right into the yard and tied their mounts to the hitch rail. Dan noticed three riders on patrol around the ranch house, Winchesters pointed to the sky. The men looked more gunslingers than drovers. Cattle were everywhere outside the yard — Texas longhorns squeezed out by other short-horn breeds, bawling and snorting to remind Dan of a trail drive. He reckoned there were still plenty of longhorns over in Texas.

Inside the foyer, a Navajo woman about fifty led the way down a hall with stairs on the left. A pair of bouncy, pre-teen girls came bounding down the steps wearing party dresses and light blue ribbons in their blonde hair.

A fine-looking woman in green followed them. 'Slow down, girls, you'll trip.' She looked at Dan and the lawyer with a weak smile. 'Birthday party,' she said.

Dan and Oliver Ashby removed their hats. Sarah was a woman in her early thirties with an innocent face that looked ten years younger, not only lovely but vulnerable. Her eyes were deep, dark-blue, the color duplicated in the girls. A delicate hand extended when she reached the bottom of the stairs. 'Welcome to our home. I'm Sarah Deller. Zack is expecting you in the den.'

Dan took the hand as gently as he could. 'J.J. Jordan,' he said.

The girls were out the front door, chased by the Navajo woman. Sarah Deller followed.

From another room a booming voice said, 'That you, Ashby? The rider musta told you. I said not to bring him. Get in here.'

Dan felt a grip on his heart. Fingers of his right hand twitched, the tips touched lightly on the hammer thong of the Peacemaker. He felt a flutter across his chest — he briefly wondered if it would be here and now. He swallowed hard.

The den was finished in dark wood with books along three walls, the fourth mostly window looking toward the silver mine hills. The floor polished, spread with a purple, Asian rug, four polished wood arm chairs and a desk built of some exotic timber. Dan resisted the urge to unhook the gun hammer thong. His forehead tingled with realization. The man stood before him behind the desk. Glasses with gray lenses, portly, thinning hair, chubby hands — robber and killer — now wealthy, solid citizen married to a beautiful mother of two pretty girls. He had swindled a silver mine from them. No question now. Monte Steep, a rebel deserter that shot Jordan Quint dead along a Texas trail leading to Waco

— Monte Steep, now calling himself Zack Deller. And Dan saw the final nail in the coffin when he looked at the desk top.

There it was.

On the desk sat a small tin box with a copper top. A princess crown had been etched in.

Foolishly, Dan started planning logistics. Gun down Steep in the den. He'd have to shoot the lawyer too. Those gunslingers outside would hear the shots and come running. He might get two before he caught bullets. No way of knowing how many there were. He'd never make the hall, never get to Mesa.

Besides, Mandy Lee had to be there, she had to be part of it.

Oliver Ashby said, 'I'm sorry, Mr Deller, but the man says he has two million dollars.'

Deller glared at Dan. 'You're wasting your time, Jordan. The Sarah D mine ain't for sale now, and it ain't never going to be for sale.' He frowned. 'Are you all right? What's so interesting about my desk?'

'Exotic wood,' Dan said.

'It was here when I got the place. Don't know nothing about it. You made a wasted trip. Can I at least offer you a glass of bourbon?'

'Not today,' Dan said. 'You got trouble coming.'

Ashby and Deller stared at him. Then Ashby nodded. 'He's talking Apache.'

Deller shook his head. 'Them stragglers are always gawking at the town. Ain't nothing to it. What did you see? Five? Six?'

Dan said, 'Eight. Just thought it might be something.'

Zack Deller — Monte Steep stood stiff with a wrinkled, fat face. 'Who the hell are you? We don't even know you. Ashby, take this jasper back to town. Look, Jordan, I'm sorry you came out here for nothing. I appreciate the warning about the Apache. But if you got a couple million or so to splurge, you get yourself another mine. The Sarah D ain't for sale.'

A light knock came on the door. Sarah opened it and took one step inside. 'The buggy is out front. We're ready to leave.'

'You ain't going no place. I don't care if she is Navajo not Apache. Those girls ain't going to her brat's party. There may be trouble. I don't like it.'

Sarah's pretty face turned pink. She stood stiff. She said, 'I have no interest at all in what you do or don't like.' She turned and slammed the door as she left.

Oliver Ashby shifted, embarrassed. 'I'm sorry Mr Deller. We shouldn't have heard that.'

Deller shrugged. 'She found out. I don't know how or from where. I think Jenny saw her in Yuma and told her. The pigeon is outta the cage now. You and me got to talk about Jenny.'

Dan said, 'I can find my own way back.'

Deller nodded. 'Yes, why don't you? Get together with Ollie here later to buy another silver claim. Like I said, my claim just ain't for sale.'

* ★ *

Less than a mile from the ranch, Dan saw a four-place buggy by the side of the road. Bundled against the cold, the two girls cried as they hugged their mama, hunched with her face in her hands, also crying. Dan rode to the buggy and stepped down.

'Trouble, ma'am?'

The girls looked at him first, their deep-blue eyes red-rimmed but clear and innocent. 'It's the man,' one of them said. 'The man from the house.'

'I'm sorry,' Sarah Deller said. 'I'm making a spectacle of myself.'

Dan stood by her seat. 'Anything I can do?'

One of the girls sniffled. 'There ain't no party. We're running away.'

'Isn't, Patricia, not ain't,' Sarah said.

'There isn't no party,' Patricia said.

248

Dan peered at the other girl. 'What's your name?'

'Judith. Mama, stop crying. We said we're going to do it, we're going to do it.'

Sarah looked up. 'Mr Jordan, please go on your way. We don't want to trouble you.'

'I'm already troubled. You can't sit out here in the cold with these girls. I can take you back to the ranch.'

'We ain't never — aren't ever going back there,' Patricia said. She was the older of the two.

'What are their ages?' Dan asked.

'Nine and eleven.'

'I'm the oldest,' Patricia said. 'That's why he picked on me.'

Dan stared at the girl, not liking the picture in his mind. He studied the three, twisted, red faces in tears looking back at him. He turned to Sarah. 'Where do you want to go?'

'Yuma,' she said. 'We have a case with a clothes change at the hotel. And a train ticket to Dodge City by way of

Sacramento. My daddy is going to meet us.' She looked behind her. 'We can't go that way. One of the men at the ranch will see the buggy.' She turned to the hitched chestnut mare. 'If we go through Darion, the marshal or some-body will come riding to tell him.'

Dan said, 'There's a trail I used when I first come out here looking for the town. Might be a little rough for the buggy, but if you're willing, I'll take you on in.'

She grabbed his arm. 'Yes. Please, Mr Jordan.' She hesitated. 'What was your business with my husband?'

'Shove on over. It ain't important, never was.' Dan tied Mesa to the back of the buggy and climbed next to her. He took the reins from her. He lightly slapped them on the back of the chestnut. 'Move it along there.'

As the buggy rolled out, Dan turned to the girls. 'Patricia, Judith, cover your ears tight. You ain't supposed to hear what I'm about to tell your mama.'

The girls squinted while they pressed

palms against their ears.

Sarah frowned. 'What is it, Mr Jordan?'

Dan said, 'My name ain't Jordan, that was my brother who your husband killed more'n fifteen years ago, back when his name was Monte Steep. He robbed banks and people and killed plenty in his time. He made some crooked deal to get that silver mine and he probably had your sister killed. I come looking for him. My name is Dan Quint and I'm here to shoot the bastard dead.'

24

In Yuma, the setting sun aimed for desert sand across the Colorado where the ferry floated next to the railroad bridge. The girls were on the train, each dressed in a plain, calico dress with bright yellow jackets, still with a ribbon in their blonde locks. Sarah Deller, in a gray suit for travel, stood in front of Dan on the station platform.

She held his arm. 'Thank you isn't enough, Dan. I don't know if I'd had the courage to do this on my own. The girls and I talked about it. He is not a kind man. With the girls growing . . . we couldn't stay there. His comments were leading to more. I have to get them away before . . . before . . . '

'Yes'm. What if he comes after you? I mean, before I get a chance to kill him.'

'My daddy will have twenty-five outriders waiting. Daddy knows why

I'm coming home. If Monte Steep enters Dodge City or the ranch, there won't be anything left for you to kill.' She stood looking at his face. 'Ida and I thought after the war we might make enough selling cattle to work the claim. Everybody northeast wanted cattle. But we couldn't afford to drive them north. We had to sell. I thought Ida and I sold the claim to Jeremiah Dickers and his partner.'

'Will Lee,' Dan said.

'Yes. I was never sure how Zack got involved — I mean, Monte Steep.'

'You gave Jeremiah Dickers a receipt for payment, didn't you?'

'Yes, the original for him, a duplicate for me. I sent it home to Dodge City for Daddy to keep.'

'Will you mail it to me, care of General Delivery here in Yuma?'

'Of course, as soon as I get there. The receipt was made out to partners, Jeremiah Dickers and William Lee.'

Dan said, 'They were already partners. They made up the paperwork before they left Missouri. Will was just bringing out his share of the money, eight thousand dollars.'

'That's half the amount Mr Dickers paid me and Ida.'

'They were going to use Will's money to operate the mine.' Dan watched the girls fuss against the train window. 'Steep had something to do with your sister's accident.'

'I wouldn't believe it but I thought so, especially after Jenny — '

Dan felt his face flush. He blinked at her. 'You saw Jenny Troup?'

'The last time I was in town. She came to me. She told me about the claim swindle, and the affair she had with Zack — Steep. So, I can add infidelity to his crimes. I might have even cared once.'

'You know where she lives?'

'No. Dan, she looks awful. She told me she's had to work as a prostitute. She's had a rough time. I gave her some money but she needs help. Will you — '

'Yes'm. I'll look her up before I go after Steep.'

'After I'm gone, he'll suspect her. He may send the marshal, or the gunfighter deputy, Orville Riker after her.'

'Yes'm,' Dan said.

Sarah stood back and studied Dan's eyes. There was something in her look. When he started to feel uncomfortable, she said, 'I've only known two real men in my life, my Daddy and my Ben. They blew my Ben to pieces in that awful, stupid war. My Daddy is getting on in years. I'm glad to know there are others — at least one other.' She hugged him then turned away and stepped up to the train car. 'I'll send you that duplicate receipt.'

Dan waited until the train was rolling across the Colorado toward California. At the coast, they would head north to Sacramento then east to Dodge City. He didn't envy the ladies that train ride, but they'd be out of the reach of Monte Steep.

Dan headed for the saloon whore-houses of Yuma.

★ ★ ★

The farce was done for. No more fancy dude duds and borrowed names. Dan Quint took back his own name and dressed in his western clothes, happy to be wearing his old Boss of the Plains Stetson again.

In the saloon, Dan felt the burn of whiskey down his throat. The bar was full of miners since it was a Saturday night, and time for some hell-raising.

The miner next to him said, 'Heard you're askin' around town about Jenny.'

'I am. You know where she is?'

'You ain't the only one looking.'

Dan nodded to the bartender, and held up two fingers. He turned back to the man. 'You work a silver claim?'

'Not the big one, one of the smaller ones down the line. Them lookin' is the lawyer and the gunslinger.'

'Orville Riker?'

'That's the jasper. So fast he dropped three in the Darion Saloon before they cleared leather. Shot all three dead. I ain't never seen nobody so fast.'

Dan finished his whiskey. 'He figure to draw down on Jenny Troup?'

'Nope, just kill her. Word is she's blabbing her mouth about things she shouldn't, works a tent out by the mines.'

'Word from who?'

The miner shrugged. 'Just word around.'

'Is Riker a sure-enough deputy marshal or does he work for the lawyer?'

'Nope. They both work for the marshal, Silver Hawthorne. Orville Riker is one of Hawthorne's deputies.' He stood tall. 'Hey, where you going?'

'To stop him,' Dan said.

*　*　*

Before Dan rode on out to the mines, he stopped at the telegraph office. He

sent one wire back east to North
Carolina.

Mandy
Come to Yuma. Stop. Found him.
Stop.
Dan

25

Dan Quint rode Mesa along the ore wagon road out to the mines. In the hotel room, he had practised. Twenty-eight draws in front of the mirror last night, and another fifty in the morning. The hand didn't freeze once. He was ready to meet Monte Steep.

He reached the mines early afternoon. Dan figured to sweep the independent ladies first, with their small tents farthest away. Larger tents held as many as four cots each, one whore per cot.

The whack of pick against rock clicked out of the mines, the Sarah D being the biggest with the most noise. The day was still too young for booze and bitches — pick axes still chipped against rock. Rock-dust haze hovered, the combined smells of male sweat and cheap perfume lingering in the air. That dust clouded the sky like a light seaside fog, coming from dark mine entrances to be whipped away high above the caverns with the wind.

From what Dan could learn, Jenny Troup had been in the business five years, a long life for a soiled dove. Always on the move, she drifted from tent to tent though she now had her own independent canvas room. She had to know others were looking for her, ordered by a man from her past — past boss, past lover. Dan left Mesa outside the tent area, tied to a broken wagon wheel. He moved on foot between small tents.

'Can I relieve some of your trouble, mister?' the girl said. She stood behind him having stepped out of a big tent, dressed in red, short and low, tiny goose bumps over her bare arms and legs.

'Jenny Troup,' Dan said, turning.

'She ain't working yet.'

'I just want conversation.'

'Mister, she got trouble you want no part of.'

'I know who's looking for her. I'm here to stop them.'

'Let me entertain you 'til she gets back. I'm Cricket.'

'Don't have the time,' he said.

Cricket appeared to shrivel a little as she glanced behind him. 'She's standing behind you with a big, nasty gun in her hand.'

'Turn around slow,' Jenny said. 'Your hand drops and I'll open a hole in you big enough a rat can crawl through.'

Cricket held her palms out. 'Jenny, I'll just go on out to a mesquite bush for a pee. You two won't miss me.'

'Go ahead,' Jenny said. 'Cowboy, I told you to turn around, slow.'

Dan turned, elbows pushing his ribs, hands out. 'I just want to talk, Jenny.'

'Start now.'

'You told Sarah Deller about Monte Steep and the silver claim swindle.'

'I never heard of Monte Steep.'

'His phony name is Zack Deller. I just put Sarah on a train for Dodge City.'

'She left him?'

'After what you told her — and what was going to happen to the girls — she had no choice.'

'Good for her.'

Jenny Troup lowered her Colt. She wore a revealing, pink saloon dress but there was nothing to her. Her dark hair hung straight past her shoulders — skinny arms and legs, triangle face with hollow cheeks and sunken, brown eyes.

'I can get you out of this life,' Dan said.

Her thin face twisted in contempt. 'Sure you can. You know how many saddle tramps say that? They can take good care of me if I just open-up only for them. Make them my one and only. And they stand without a decent horse to ride or any kind of roof. I heard it all before. Who are you?'

'Dan Quint.'

She frowned at him. 'Deadly Dan Quint, the gunfighter?'

'I've been called that.'

'And you know Sarah Deller?'

Dan looked around at the tents. 'Can we talk someplace?'

'Yeah, my place.' She led the way between canvas to the edge of them. Her small tent had no standing headroom. Inside was a cot and a table with a lantern. A sway-back gray horse with a torn saddle was tied up behind. 'It ain't luxurious but it's dump cozy.' He sat on a weathered, wooden box, she on the cot. Jenny pulled a whiskey bottle from under the cot. 'I got a couple of glasses someplace.' They too were under the cot along with a carpet bag. She poured and held out her glass. 'Here's looking up your address.' She drank half the glass in one gulp. Afternoon sun winking in the tent entrance showed her face, about thirty, with few wrinkles, but with a bone-tired, worn out, hollow weariness.

Dan threw down a slug. The stuff resembled the smell of coyote piss. 'You were the bookkeeper for Zack Deller on the claim sale.'

'And his personal piece.' She finished her glass and coughed. 'Oliver wanted some too. When I told him, pay a dollar upstairs at the Deller Waterhole, he made sure Horace found out about the affair.'

'Horace?'

'My husband — he kicked me out, then went after Oliver, and got himself shot dead. He thought I was putting out to Oliver, the fool.' She looked beyond the tent entrance, momentarily lost in memory. 'So, anyway, you know how it goes. I'm a fresh widow. Zack says I got to be nicer to Oliver. I could tell the bloom was off any romance he felt for me. It follows a pattern — first you do it for love, then you do it for a few of your lover's friends, then you do it for acquaintances, then you start getting small gifts, then some cash, and eventually you turn whore. Keep at it long enough and you're down to a dollar a poke, saving enough to buy your own tent. I got a kid someplace, Trudy; I'd like to see her again — other people raising her.' She fixed Dan with a stare. 'And you're going to take me away from all this?'

'How did you fix the books, Jenny?'

She shrugged. 'Not hard. I changed the names Jeremiah Dickers and William Lee to Zack Deller. Zack paid no money. Tore out the page and wrote on a new blank one. Zack arranged for Jeremiah to get a worthless copper claim in Aztec and told him to stay out of Yuma and Darion or else. Dickers had something over them was why he wasn't killed — some hidden papers, he said. Will Lee was still coming out with his family and they figured to take care of him when he got here. He never made it. I didn't find out until later that Ida and Sarah Collins wrote a receipt — with a duplicate.'

'Will Lee had a daughter,' Dan said. 'She's on her way. Jeremiah is dead, along with the gunfighter who threatened him.' Dan put his hand on hers. 'You know a killer is coming for you.'

'Slipper sent him, Orville Riker

265

— Oliver and Orville, what a pair. Guess Zack thinks I still know too much. Sarah was nice. She gave me some money.'

'Where do you want to go, Jenny — someplace to start over?'

'As what — another whore?'

'As a widowed mother — think you can work as a bookkeeper again, maybe in Sacramento? Nobody needs to know about this. You'll have enough to get settled.'

'I don't have money for the train ride or any life like that.'

'We'll get you outfitted, some decent clothes, help you get your daughter — where is she?'

'Santa Fe.'

'You can go to Sacramento from there.'

Jenny squinted at him. 'How will I pull that off? Anybody can see I'm worn out as a rodeo bronc.'

'You got a horse?'

She jerked her head. 'The tired old gray I keep tied behind the tent here.'

'We'll get you healthy — make you eat good, get you ready, you can study the work.'

'Who's we?'

'Will's daughter, Mandy Lee — and me. She'll have the mine. We'll get it done. Right now I got to get you away from these mines.'

She grimaced, doubt showing over her face. 'I need money, Dan.'

'I got fifty dollars for you. That'll keep you for a week.'

'Where?'

'Aztec — it's where they stuck Jeremiah Dickers. The tent is still there. I'll kick out anybody nesting in it.'

Shaking her head, she said, 'I don't know, Dan. What about Orville Riker, the killer deputy Slipper is sending — and Oliver Ashby?'

'They come looking for you, what they'll get is me.'

26

In Yuma, Dan checked with Western Union. The wire was there. While Jenny waited in the buckboard, he rolled his own and lit up by Mesa with his elbows on the saddle. He felt a knot in his chest and a weakness to his knees, not knowing what was in the message. Dan unfolded the paper.

Dan
Roger and I reach Yuma Sunday a
week. Stop. Western Pacific 2:35.
Stop. He has plan.
Mandy

With gritted teeth, Dan crumpled the paper message to a tight ball. He squinted at the buckboard wheel and breathed a deep breath, then tossed the ball into the back of the wagon. She was bringing Roger. And Roger had a plan.

Jenny watched him closely. 'Bad news?' she asked.

'Might be. Let's get on to Aztec.'

Weather held good to Aztec. A couple of grizzled copper miners nested in Jeremiah Dickers' tent with a chunky, granny whore called Sleepy Sue. They grumbled with threats but moved out peaceable enough, no gunfire necessary. Sleepy Sue asked to stay. Jenny was okay with that as long as they didn't practice the trade. Sleepy Sue told them she figured to be retired anyway seeing as how she was toothless, old, fat and ugly, with a face as lumpy and puffed and gray as rain clouds. She did like the look of the frail Jenny though.

Dan reckoned the old whore liked Jenny's fifty dollars more. He told her if she treated Jenny right and didn't let the old miners back in the tent, she'd be taken care of. He gave her two five-dollar gold pieces on account. He let them keep Rowdy along with the tired gray.

Sleepy Sue acted as if she saw a

sunny, bright future in the arrangement.

★ ★ ★

In the Darion Saloon, Dan waited at the bar, tossing down too many quarter whiskeys. He had heard the marshal was out at the ranch. He hoped that when they returned, Zack Deller — Monte Steep, would be with them. His mind churned and his belly knotted. He would deal with the polecats himself — without help, and without some damned plan.

Zack Deller stayed at the ranch. While the moon raised high, Marshal Slipper Hawthorne, Attorney Oliver Ashby and Deputy Orville Riker rode back into Darion.

As expected they went to the Deller Waterhole first, the higher-class saloon, asking around loudly, wanting to know where Jenny Troup got herself off to, and who took her there. Nobody knew where, but they knew who. And Dan stood with his boot on the brass rail across the road in the Darion Saloon, where pickaxe miners, drifter saddle tramps, dollar whores, low-life bums and watered whiskey waited.

Dan figured saloon drinkers didn't know why the whore Jenny Troup had to be killed, just that she had done something to irritate the man who owned the town, and she had to go. Nobody crossed Zack Deller — except the latest word was his good-looking wife took her sweet little girls and got herself on a train out of Arizona — and that had to be enough to make a preacher piss on a stranger.

Dan reckoned he should have eaten something, while he watched through the batwing doors as two men came out and started across the street — Oliver and Orville. The marshal stayed behind. Drinkers knew what was coming. They gave Dan a five-foot space all around as they shuffled away. They wouldn't leave because they didn't want to miss any action. Stray bullets always hit somebody else.

Behind him, toward the end of the bar, the saloon keeper said, 'You bust my mirror, you buy it.'

Dan waited some more, the thong off the hammer.

The pair stepped out of darkness to the boardwalk — the lawyer walked kind of dainty, the deputy stomped determinedly.

Oliver's voice carried inside. 'Damn it, we're going to talk to the man, ask him what he did with her.' His suit looked rumpled; his derby had cocked a little to one side. He squirmed to the bat wings. 'He can't tell us nothing if you shoot him dead.'

The lawyer's sidekick clomped ahead, leaning into his boots with each stomp. 'Ain't gonna be much talk.' His vest was food-stained but had a bright deputy star on it. The gray ten-gallon Stetson had frayed around the brim, a big, splashy pattern bandana almost covered his chest but not enough to hide the badge. The Peacemaker Colt

.45 bounced with the step up. The eyes were dark slits.

He led the way, swinging through the doors.

'Mr Quint,' Ashby said. 'We're looking — '

'No talk,' Orville Riker said. He reached the centre of the room just as the .45 slug tore into his left eye. His ten-gallon hat jerked forward as his head snapped back. A second shot went through his heart.

The lawyer pulled a small revolver from inside his jacket and fired once as a bullet ripped into his stomach.

Dan felt a burning fire from the slug under his arm as it tore skin and chipped a rib bone. He fell back against the bar and dropped to one knee. He took his time and shot the attorney through the top of the head. Ashby's revolver had already dropped to the floor.

Dan stood slowly and holstered the Peacemaker. He squeezed his right arm against his stinging side and looked around the saloon. Nobody moved much. He pushed away from the bar and stepped over the bleeding deputy to walk out the batwing doors, leaving them swinging behind him.

PART THREE

LOVE AND FRIENDS

27

With a torn-strip, hotel pillow case tied tight, Dan made it to the doc in Yuma on Mesa. Other than removing bone fragments and sewing a few stitches and a new bandage wrap for the chipped rib, there wasn't much the doc could do. He told Dan to stay in bed a few days.

Dan lasted in the Yuma hotel room until Saturday noon. After breakfast, he rode out to Aztec and the tent. Jenny and Sleepy Sue looked just fine. Somewhere in Aztec, they had found proper women's clothes. They each had a bath, did things with each other's hair, swept up the tent, and offered Dan fresh coffee made with real, ground coffee beans, no acorns or other nuts or berries. They listened while Dan recalled the Darion gunfight with the deputy and the lawyer.

Jenny was pleased about the recently deceased lawyer, Oliver Ashby, but she felt sorry Dan got himself shot. Dan reckoned Jenny might pass for under thirty. Folks might take her for a bookkeeper. Sleepy Sue looked like a matronly old maid fussing over Jenny.

Dan was so impressed he told the ladies he was hitching the wagon. They'd be staying at the hotel in Yuma tonight. When the train got in Sunday, they'd all be heading out to Darion for one last bit of business before the move to Santa Fe. Jenny paced the tent, wringing her hands. She turned nervous about going back to Yuma. She thought anybody would easily know her for a whore. A few of the gents might even recognize her. Dan told her she looked like a bookkeeper and to keep thinking she looked like a bookkeeper.

When they were in Yuma, Dan got another room for the ladies, and rented a spare room for Mandy. Mr Farnsworth could take care of himself. Down in the stables he bought a gelding, figuring to hitch it and the tired gray to Jenny's old buckboard. Mandy would ride Rowdy beside Mesa. The brilliant young lawyer would be in the wagon with the freshly-converted ladies if he didn't care for riding horses.

Back in his hotel room, Dan Quint girded himself for another meeting with Mandy Lee.

*   *   *

The Western Pacific train squeaked and hissed into the Yuma station at 2:51 Sunday. Disembarking passengers brought with them the smell of cross-country travel. Only children appeared giggly — little girls apparently loved to scream. Adults showed themselves to be more determined than unhappy. A few traveled as a way of life. Their faces held life experience, days and nights with few surprises, yet rich in varied events. The train itself brought a life — the hot burning of steel wheels on steel ribbon tracks, cigar and pipe smoke of men, women's perfume, leather suitcases, a different holster-leather smell coupled with oiled revolvers — coal fire to build up steam, steam hissing out and up the stack — a buzz of conversations from those who arrived and greeters — ladies in bustles, men with handlebar mustaches, beards and derbies — a few cowboys carrying saddles.

Jenny Troup and Sleepy Sue had been shopping and were unwrapping and packing in their hotel room. All they had purchased went into new carpet bags.

Dan had left them, and went to wait on the platform. He felt no real, physical flutter or tingle, he felt anticipation, as if jumping and waiting to land on something dark, not knowing what it was, whether it slanted or was soft or wet or hard as a train wheel. The feeling was not much different from stepping into a gunfight.

The couple emerged from the car

and down train steps to the platform — a young couple — the man irritated, the lady searching. Dan looked at her and kept looking at her and liked looking at her, and knew he wanted her. She didn't see him. They were little more than three arm's-length away in a crowd.

Roger Farnsworth, dressed without a wrinkle, fresh shaved, tall and handsome with stovetop hat said, 'With all the money the railroad makes you'd think they might be on time.'

'Where is he?' she said. She belonged in a store window for the latest fashion. She wore a dark-blue hooped dress, tight through the waist and bodice, white gloves, a funny hat — her green eyes searched, she used her gloved hand to shade her eyes against the glare of the sun, flawless skin, beautiful — an angel.

Dan felt his heart squeeze when he almost caught her gaze, then drop through a hangman's trap door when Roger Farnsworth moved beside her.

His arm circled her tiny waist and he pulled her tight against him in a gesture of possession. She didn't resist until she locked eyes with Dan's.

Her face brightened to a happy smile. 'Dan,' she said softly. 'My Dan.' She pulled away from the young man and with two steps had wrapped her arms around Dan's neck and pushed against him.

She felt far too good. He held her outline tighter for longer than he felt he should. His rib offered some protest. When he released her, she clung for a few seconds longer, and that pleased him.

'I have a room for you,' he said to her.

Roger came forward grabbing his hand, 'Good to see you again, Quint. We have much to discuss.'

'Roger!' Mandy said in irritation.

Roger ignored her, concentrating on Dan. 'Did you locate Jenny Troup? You must understand she is the key.'

Now Dan kept his arm circled

possessively around Mandy's waist. 'She's waiting in a hotel room.'

'Here?' Roger stiffened. He blinked. 'Here in town?'

'Right here in downtown Yuma.'

'But . . . but . . . I hope you haven't messed everything up, Quint. You were just supposed to locate her. Just locate her. Let those who know these procedures take charge. My plan is to — '

Dan ignored him. He looked down at Mandy's face. 'Let's go.'

Roger Farnsworth put his hand on Dan's shoulder. 'Now — '

Dan stiffened, and spun toward him, and said, 'Don't do that.'

Farnsworth jerked his hand back when he saw Dan's eyes. 'I've already made reservations — in fact I've made arrangements for a buggy too — for the ride to Darion.'

Mandy had her head on Dan's chest. She looked up to his eyes. 'Why a room for me?'

'I definitely didn't want you to have one with him.'

'Don't you have intentions for me?'

'Yes'm, I sure do.'

'I think they flow along with the ideas I have for you. It's been long enough, Dan.'

'Yes'm, it has.'

'There's the buggy,' Roger Farnsworth said. He appeared to be off in his world of plans. 'Mandy, shall we get the luggage?' As he was about to head out, he turned to Dan. 'I need to talk to you.'

'It all flows in good time,' Dan said. He took Mandy's elbow. 'You get the luggage, Roger, while I introduce Mandy to Jenny Troup.'

'Wait,' Farnsworth said.

But Dan and Mandy had already started across the road to the hotel.

★　★　★

After dinner, they went to Jenny and Sleepy Sue's room for Riesling wine and talk. Dan brought Roger and Mandy up to date on current events.

284

Jenny took a liking to the wine and wondered if any might be available in Sacramento. Her animated gestures made her seem to come alive. Talking with Mandy about subjects other than the trade left Dan with no doubt Jenny would do well in Sacramento. Santa Fe, first.

But before that came Darion.

Enough chairs had been brought in for everyone. Roger arranged it. Sleepy Sue preferred to sit on the edge of the bed. She gazed from one to another, her lumpy face passive. Roger sat next to Mandy so he could hold her hand. Dan sat across from her so he got a full view of her, silly hat to cute shoes.

Roger said, 'Are you all right, sweetheart.'

'Better than all right, Roger.'

'It's just that — now and then you shiver. Are you cold?'

'I'll get over it. I'm sure I'll get over it.'

Roger patted her hand. 'I know it's a

different climate. Shall I get you a wrap? A coat?'

'Maybe it's anticipation. I know a cure will come.'

Roger nodded. 'Yes, the excitement.' He sighed deeply. 'Now that we're out here and have seen Dan again, I think it is time for you and I to talk about our future.'

Mandy looked at him with a frown. She glanced across at Dan then continued her frown for Roger.

Dan said, 'About Monte Steep, I already know what's gonna happen.'

Roger stood. 'Quint, that's just the one thing that can't happen. He must be — '

Sleepy Sue said, 'Like hell, it won't. I ain't havin' my Jenny hurt no more. Nobody is huntin' her down.'

Farnsworth pointed a bony finger at her. 'You stay out of this. It has nothing to do with you.' He frowned. 'Who *are* you, anyway?'

Jenny's little face scrunched up in agony. She wrung her hands. 'Dan?'

286

'Don't concern yourself, girl,' Dan said.

She leaned forward. 'Straighten this out, Dan. Fix it.'

Dan turned to Farnsworth. 'Monte Steep is dead. Ain't no part of your plan affects that.'

Still standing in the middle of the room, Farnsworth said, 'Listen to me, Quint. I'm not having my girl dragged into some Wild West gunfight.'

'It ain't up to you, lawyer-boy, and you better make sure she's your girl, first.'

Farnsworth spun toward Mandy, 'Tell him, my love.'

Mandy sighed. 'Roger, I never hid my feelings from you.'

'But, that was before. My God, look at him. He can't even move right.'

Sleepy Sue said, 'That's 'cause he got shot up some in a gun-fight. He's healing.'

Mandy was on her feet. 'Dan?'

Sleepy Sue glared at Roger. 'Who the hell is *you*, boy?'

287

Mandy knelt in front of Dan, her lovely face full of concern. 'Why didn't you tell me?'

'I was gettin' to it.' He looked up at Roger. 'There ain't nothin' wrong with your plan, Roger, it's jest I already got it worked out. That duplicate receipt I told you about oughta be here any day, mebbe tomorrow. That shot-dead lawyer has got books in his office we got to bust in and get, and jiggle some entries around. There's army troops outside Darion 'cause they expecting an Apache attack.' He cupped Mandy's chin at his knees. 'No, me and this little girl here got a score to settle from a past you may know about but don't really understand. That ain't changin'. We got to escort these two ladies to Santa Fe to get Jenny's daughter so she can head on out to Sacramento.' He turned to Sleepy Sue. 'I reckon Jenny will have help raisin' the girl.'

Jenny and Sleepy Sue exchanged looks. Jenny nodded vigorously.

'Mandy,' Roger said. 'Do you go

along with this?'

Mandy slowly turned away from Dan and gave Roger a steady stare. 'Dan pretty much talks for me, Roger.'

'Me too,' Jenny said.

'And me,' Sleepy Sue said.

Roger Farnsworth sank into his chair. He put his elbows on his knees and his chin on his hands. 'What about you and me, Mandy? I have that buggy to take us to Darion.'

'I can't tell you anything about you and me.'

'We'll talk tonight. I'll come to your room.'

Mandy put her hand on Dan's knee. 'I have a feeling I'll be busy tonight. In the morning, I'll tell you everything you need to know.'

28

Past midnight she opened her door for him. She wore only a thin nightgown and her brown-copper hair was down. She didn't stand in the doorway. Leaving the door ajar she walked to the center of the room and stood waiting.

She shivered as he closed the door and crossed to her.

Her hands slid up his arms and around his neck. 'I've waited too long.'

'Just long enough,' he said. 'Almost too long.'

'I was so afraid coming here.'

'Why?'

'Rejection — I thought you might leave me empty again.'

'Would that have sent you to Roger?'

'I'm not sure. He's been so good to me — as a friend. I know he expected that eventually he'd — '

'He worships you, girl.'

'I know.'

'He thinks you belong to him.'

'You know who I belong to, who I've always belonged to. You were just too dumb to see it.'

'Mebbe, but I ain't too dumb to show it.'

He gathered her body close and kissed her the way she needed to be kissed. He swept her off her feet and carried her to the bed. He held no hesitation, no doubt, none at all.

'At last,' she whispered.

★　★　★

The pain in his rib woke him. Her face snuggled against his throat. Long, copper hair sprayed across his face. He wanted to be sure that she really was stretched beside him with her long, slim, naked leg over his stomach. He explored her with his palms, every inch of her sleek curves. She had brought her natural beauty to him with passionate abandon.

When he moved slightly toward the edge of the bed, she grumbled.

She said, 'Don't you dare leave my bed before I'm done with you.'

'What can you want me for now?'

'More, Deadly Dan Quint. You don't just boil up this hidden passion then push on out of bed.'

He turned back to her with his hands on her shoulders. He pushed her down under him. 'All right then.'

'That's better,' she said with a grin.

* * *

She lay without clothes beside him with her knees drawn up. 'It's almost noon. Don't you get hungry for something besides me?'

'I might, eventually.'

'God, Dan. Why did you make me wait so long? I know you've been with many women. You're very experienced.'

'How would you know that?'

'Are you disappointed I have none?'

292

'Not at all. You have a natural passion.'

'Have all your other women been experienced?'

'Yes.'

'You'll have to teach me.' She turned against him making him grimace with a stab of rib pain. She jerked up. 'I didn't even think — I'm so sorry, Dan. And with all the things we did — Oh Dan, it must have been awful for you, the pain.'

'It sure wasn't awful, it was delicious.'

Her cheeks flushed. She put her index finger on his lips, 'Hush.' Her cheek went to his chest. 'I've never felt so — so explosive. It was wonderful. Are you going to marry me? In Santa Fe?'

'Yes.'

'I'll have Jenny to stand up with me.' She frowned. 'You won't have a Best Man.'

'Sleepy Sue can be my Best Man.'

That made her chuckle. 'You're right. The marriage is more important than the ceremony. Do you want to come back here to live?'

'No.'

'Will we go with Jenny and Sleepy Sue to Sacramento?'

Dan kissed her forehead. Now he regretted the lost time, all those years. He still thought she had been too young, yet he regretted the years they weren't together. 'Washington Territory,' he said.

'Yes,' she said. 'We don't need to be rich.'

Dan said, 'You'll have the mining claim to start with.'

'I'll sell that. We'll find something up in the Northwest, up in Washington Territory where we can live a happy life together.'

'You'll be in charge of that.'

'Of certain parts, yes.'

'You know we got something to do first.'

'Monte Steep. He's the last one left. On the train coming out here, he was all I thought of — well, when I wasn't aching for you. What did you say he calls himself now?'

'Zack Deller.'

'And his family left him?'

'Went back home to Kansas, wife and two girls.'

'Then there's just him.'

'And his marshal.'

'Enough for the two of us. I've been practising again, Dan. Roger was upset but I want to be as fast as you, like before.'

'That won't be hard these days.'

She sat with her knees under her. 'We best get started. I'm ready. I'm ready to tell Roger we want him with us for the paperwork in Darion and the duplicate receipt and for him to get with a judge so it's all legal. And I'm ready to tell him, he can forget about any kind of romance with me. I've been taken well and I'm spoken for.'

'Maybe he'll buy the silver claim.'

Her eyebrows went up. 'You know, I'll offer it to him. But after the paper is legal.' She kissed him well on the lips. 'I'm eager to get started, love.'

'Why so eager?'

'Haven't you heard, Mr Quint? I'm a satisfied woman now. If I were to die tomorrow it would be as a real woman, not an innocent girl.'

* * *

Roger Farnsworth did not take the news well. What surprised Dan was why Famsworth took it at all. He had to have known. The boy was highly educated but with minimal real-life experience — book smart, life dumb. Likely, the lad knew little, if any, woman experience. Dan had known Mandy since she was twelve. He knew her spirit and temper and capacity for life. He'd always figured her with a real man, certainly — and with eventual heart-wrenching regret — not a man as age advanced and battered as himself, but never with a boy like Roger Farnsworth. Despite Dan's handicaps, the beautiful, angelic, young woman had chosen and given herself to him.

That was the end of it. She was his now and deadly, bad news to anyone who tried to change that. He loved a grand woman who loved him back, not for what he represented, but for him, including the shot-to-pieces carcass and cranky disposition. She owned every part of him; he had nothing left for anybody else.

Any thought of rolling to Darion on Monday ended when Roger and Mandy had lunch alone together. Without believing her, Roger went from the lunch table, out of the hotel to the downtown saloon bar.

Dan was in the stable about to hitch the buckboard when Mandy ran to him and threw her arms around his neck.

'Roger is in the saloon. I'm afraid he'll find trouble. I tried to stop him.'

Dan dropped the harness over a wood peg and patted her back. 'Does he carry a gun?'

Mandy pushed away. 'Yes, a small revolver in a belly holster.'

Dan unhooked the thong off the

Peacemaker hammer. 'I'll look into it.'

As he started for the stable door headed toward the saloon, Mandy grabbed his arm.

'Dan, you won't hurt him. You can't hurt him. Please.'

'That's up to Farnsworth,' Dan said, pulling away.

29

Roger Farnsworth tossed down a glass of cheap bar whiskey like a lad without experience tossing down cheap bar whiskey. It wasn't his first. When Dan walked in, Roger stood at the bar, his polished east coast boot planted on the brass rail but slipping off on occasion. A cowboy stood to his left, Stetson brim pulled low in front of his eyes — he stared at his whiskey glass like a man agonizing over a broken heart. To Roger's right, two business types in suits without hats, bent together as if in conspiracy. Upstairs, girls still slept off Sunday night.

Monday afternoon brought little downtown saloon action.

Dan stepped to the bar and nodded to the bar keep. 'Another for my friend.'

Roger bobbed and turned to Dan. 'You're not my friend, Dan Quint.'

Dan said, 'We were headed for Darion today.'

'To hell with Darion. To hell with you.' He turned to his full glass and bent his head. 'To hell with Mandy Lee.'

'Careful, Farnsworth. You can feel sorry for yourself on your own two-bits. Things got to be done.' He tossed down his whiskey, nodded with two fingers up.

'I had a plan — how to get her set for life.'

'I ain't got no plan, just stuff got to be done. Mandy is already set for life.'

Farnsworth snapped to attention. 'You say her name, like, familiar, like you know her well, too well. How dare you say her name like that. Who do you think you are?'

'The chosen one.'

'She told me she was with you last night.'

'She was.'

He stood stiff and stared, his stovepipe hat cocked a little to the side,

300

his thin face beet-red with drink and rage. 'You took her to your bed?'

'No, she took me to her bed.'

'Liar!'

Dan moved a little away from the bar so his right hand was free of obstacles.

Roger blinked and looked hard at Dan's gun hand. 'Do you intend to shoot me?'

'If I have to. I take into consideration you're twisted around and upset so I ain't gonna want to. You keep on the trail you're driving and you'll force me. I don't know you, not close as a friend like Mandy. To me you're just an arrogant, pompous little ass. I won't want to but you keep prodding with insults about the lady and me and you can't accept the way of life or what she really wants, and I'll drop you where you stand.'

'You mean get me out of your path?'

'You ain't in my path no more, but that's one way to remove your presence completely.'

Roger's bony shoulders slumped

inside the dark coat. He turned back to the bar and sipped whiskey. 'You aware how many years I've known her?'

'Not near as many as me.'

He nodded. 'And now you've been . . . intimate with her.'

'That I have. It was bound to happen. You shoulda seen it coming. Now I'm gonna marry the woman and impregnate her soon as I can.'

'God! I can't even think of her with you, some prairie gunfighter, old enough to be her daddy.'

'Start.'

'I . . . just can't.'

'Then wrap your thinking around this. She ain't never gonna be with you. Set that heavy in your head.'

'What am I to do?'

'Everything you was gonna do with her only without her. It's the trail I was gonna take.'

Roger squinted sideways at Dan. 'You weren't sure?'

'I ain't never been sure. She admires you and considers you a good friend. I didn't know how she really thought or felt. She mighta chose you. She talks high enough about you. But I'm sure now. You can bet your last gold piece how sure I am.'

'But . . . her education — she might have been a fine attorney.'

'She still might.'

'No, you'll have her campfire-cooking in some tepee, barefoot and pregnant.'

'It'll be her choice. Wherever she is, she'll wake mornings with a smile.'

Roger Farnsworth shook his head. 'That's that then.'

'So, do I got to shoot you down or are you walking away or are we gonna get on with the business we got.'

'You mean making Mandy rich.'

'And other stuff.'

★   ★   ★

The two men walked together to the Post Office and Dan claimed the duplicate receipt in General Delivery sent from Sarah Deller. Sarah had included a short note.

Dan. Home safe. Make things right. Luck. Sarah.

Dan handed the receipt to Roger Farnsworth.

He read it twice as they walked back to the hotel. 'This might be enough in itself. What illegal activity do you have in mind when we reach Darion?'

'Do what they did. Break into the lawyer's office, tear out the old page, replace it with a new entry and a new claim form. Make it all the same only with Jeremiah Dickers and Will Lee as owners. With them deceased, Mandy inherits.'

'Then what? Mandy becomes a silver mine owner? She settles here?'

They stopped in the hotel lobby. Dan said, 'We got other ideas. Want to buy it?'

'Buy what, the silver mine?'

'I hear it's a money maker.'

Roger was silent for a spell. 'You think I want to live out here in the Wild West?'

'Some say it's the future of the country.'

'Me, owning a silver mine.'

'You're rich enough. You could be one of them absentee owners.'

But Roger stared at the swirls in the royal blue, hotel lobby carpet. 'No, I'd want my own hand in running it.'

'You can make some plans about it. Don't count on support from Darion.'

'Why not?'

'Any day now, I think the Apache are gonna reduce it to ashes and rubble.'

★   ★   ★

When Dan entered Mandy's room he felt swept back years to when a girl rode the southwest and Dakota trails with him.

Mandy Lee stood in front of the mirror with her hair tied at her neck and a Plains Stetson on her head. She wore tight buckskin and a linen shirt. The Colt Navy .36 was strapped to her slim hip.

305

For an instant, he had a memory flash — of the Republican River in Kansas.

She turned to Dan. 'Draw on me.'

'No.'

'Where is Roger?'

'Pondering a few things.'

'You didn't do anything?'

'No, we talked.'

'Thank you for not shooting him.'

'That still might be dangling out there.'

'Don't say that, Dan.'

'Or, he might buy your silver claim.'

She worked her lips to a whimsical smile. 'I see a look in your eye.'

'It ain't got nothing to do with drawing guns or Roger Farnsworth.'

'You like the fit of the buckskin, don't you?'

'I do.'

'Well, if you're not going to draw, why don't you come over here and kiss me?'

'Why don't I?'

'You see, I didn't make up the bed.'

'No need to.'

'Aren't we on our way to Darion today?'

'First thing in the morning.' He took a step toward her.

She hooked her thumbs over her gun belt and pushed her shoulders back. 'Maybe you'd better do something about me.'

'Maybe I'd better,' he said as he wrapped his arm around her waist and pulled her close.

Her lips melted into his kiss.

30

The last day of November, 1880, during an icy sunrise, the small parade rolled out of Yuma along the trail Dan had taken to bring Sarah and the girls from the ranch to the train station. Dan rode Mesa, Mandy, Rowdy, both wearing heavy buffalo coats. The gelding and gray pulled the buckboard with a bundled Sleepy Sue holding reins and Jenny Troup on the splintered seat, and everybody's worldly possessions canvas-wrapped in back. Roger Farnsworth brought up the rear in his fresh-bought two-seat buggy. He had exchanged his stovepipe hat for a beaver cap — saying that was as frontier as he intended to get.

Walking the horses, Mandy said, 'What if Steep ain't at the ranch?'

'We'll go where he is.'

She held the saddle-horn tight with

both gloved hands. 'I dreamed of my folks last night.'

Dan looked at her. 'Are you sure you're ready?'

'Anticipation,' she said, 'more than waiting for you to make me a woman. We've been after him a long time, Dan.'

'A long time,' Dan said. 'Do you still pine for him dead?'

'Yes, as much as before. I had a period when I was caught up in the social part of school. I thought it might be too late. No, he dies. You and me kill him, Dan. That's the way of it'

'Roger wants him punished. He should be in Yuma Territorial.'

'I still picture our little wagon and what he and his gang did. And I keep thinking of my ma, and then I think of Sarah and her little girls. She had to do what she did.'

'I was glad to help.'

'She was a brave woman. You and I know what the animal is capable of.'

Dan sighed. 'Not much longer.'

'No, not much longer.'

When they reached the ranch, Dan saw no riders. Cattle bawled beyond the out buildings, some in the yard.

Still on the trail outside the gate, Dan said to Sleepy Sue at the reins of the buckboard, 'You wait out here. Me and Mandy will have a look-see.'

While Mandy tied Rowdy's reins to the post, Dan walked around the main building, peering in windows. Mandy knocked on the door, her hand on the grip of the Navy .36. Dan saw no movement. He came around to the front and waited just long enough for her to move aside before he kicked in the door. The splintered wood noise cracked across the backs of grazing cattle. He waved his arm to the buckboard and buggy and went inside. Mandy followed across the foyer to the den. Through the doorway, Dan led her to the desk.

'There it is,' he said pointing to the little, tin box.

Mandy picked it up and opened the copper top. She held it to her breast and stared into it. 'Oh, Dan,' she said with a catch in her throat. Her tears dropped to the little box while she stared. She sniffled. Her wet, green eyes looked up at Dan. 'We're wasting time.'

Before they left the buckboard and buggy there in the yard, Dan opened all the ranch yard gates to let the cattle wander free.

'Let the Apache have them,' he said.

* * *

Dan heard gunshots and war-whoops a quarter mile before he and Mandy reached Darion. The trail entered from the southeast. Apaches attacked from west and north, more than thirty braves, faces painted for war. Wagon and furniture barriers stretched across the main road with men hunched behind them, guns drawn. Town-skirting tents already burned. Cavalry soldiers mounted and rode back and forth, firing at random. Dan stayed away from the main road. He led Mandy along the back of the office building. The saloon was the first of the structures across the road to burst into flames. Apaches rode, firing as they went, naked from the waist up, dropping blue bellies, lighting buildings off.

Dan dismounted behind the office building. Mandy followed him to the door. More structures ignited. A staccato of shots repeated up and down the main road. Men behind barriers shot Apaches down from their mounts. With his shoulder, Dan busted in the door. The rib shot his side with pain. The tents had now burned to ashes. Smoke waved with the wind across the roofs of the few structures standing. A gang of ten Apaches rode the main road killing and scalping anyone in front of them. The screams of victims joined the battle-whoops. Five to seven white men were left, fighting and dying under orders from mine owners and without spirit.

Up stairs, Dan led Mandy along the office door's hallway. They jerked as a window shattered at the end of the hall with a shot. A torch crashed through and ignited the unpainted wall.

When Dan reached the lawyer's office he tried the door knob. It was locked. 'I got a key,' he said. He stood back and shot his boot heel against the knob. Wood splintered with a crack as the door burst open.

Mandy went in first. 'Everybody from the ranch must be in town,' she said.

'Won't do no good.'

The room was dark, only wavy scarlet firelight from down the hall showed objects. Dan went around the desk to the polished wood filing cabinet. A brass padlock hung on the front latch. He pulled his Peacemaker and swung the grip to break open the lock. Mandy slid out the drawer and began rifling files.

She pulled a file labeled, *Sarah D*, and opened it. 'The claim and deed are here. There's a ledger.'

'Take the whole thing.'

Flames began eating through the wall. Mandy started for the splintered door, shoving the folder down the front of her gun belt. 'Where is he? You think he's outside fighting?'

'Not likely,' Dan said. 'He's got an office next door.'

Flames crept along the opposite hall wall.

Dan started around the desk. Rapid fire and whoops came from just outside, visible through a burned-out wall. The main road showed only smoke and flame now with riding, painted, shirtless men firing at anything that moved. Cavalry came in from the west, about five left, shooting and getting shot. Most men behind the wagons were dead. All buildings burned. Choking smoke curled inside the office, hugging the ceiling. Dan coughed.

In front of the wall of flame outside the door, Monte Steep's chunky suit filled the office doorway. He had a file under his arm. His pudgy face widened in surprise. The file fell as he reached for his gun. 'Jordan!' he shouted.

Dan started to draw. His forearm tingled and lost feeling — down to his thumb. His hand went numb. The Colt dropped to the floor as Steep fired. Dan felt a hammer-blow to his chest. He twisted and went down to one knee. He felt a blade twisting inside his rib cage, pain driving him farther down. More smoke curled in to blur his vision.

Steep fired again but missed. He swung his gun around as Mandy shot him in the chest then quickly again through the neck. Steep jerked back through the open door and fell to the floor of the hall, the timber already beginning to burn.

Another shot was fired from out of sight, the bullet hit the doorjamb. Slipper Hawthorne knelt at the door, both hands filled with guns. He fired at Mandy. She jumped back. By then Dan had feeling back in his hand. His chest pain spread to his back. He felt fear, not for himself but for Mandy. More pain squeezed through his chest. He gritted his teeth and grimaced against it. The pain through his chest drove clear thinking from his head. His legs started to go numb. The Colt came off the floor, the hammer cocked. Slipper was set upon by a coughing spell and fired wild. Dan shot Slipper in the left knee, then the stomach, then the chest. Dan forced himself to his feet as Hawthorne fell forward, his hat gone, short muddy hair smeared with blood. Dan shot him again through the back of the head.

Mandy fell to her hands and knees beside the desk and vomited. Smoke crawling into her lungs made her cough. She rolled away with a short gagging fit and sat with her legs out, leaning against the file cabinet, shaking her head.

Out in the hall with the floor fire creeping toward Monte Steep, he moved his leg. The dark eyes in his flabby face blinked.

Mandy grabbed the desk top and

pushed to her feet. The upper left arm of the buffalo coat was bleeding. 'Dan?' she said.

'He's still breathing,' Dan said. He sat on the corner of the desk holding his chest, the Colt aimed at Steep.

Mandy came around the desk to the doorway, her Navy .36 aimed at Steep's bleeding head.

Steep frowned at her. 'Who . . . ?'

Mandy said, 'You don't remember. A smoldering wagon in the rain, southwest of here. The Lee family — my pa Will Lee, my ma Elizabeth, my little brother Willy, me a twelve-year-old girl hidden under the wagon. You killed them and used my ma for fun. Dan rode in before you found me. You stole my pa's silver claim from Jeremiah Dickers — the tin box with the copper top.' She raised her Colt. 'Yes, you remember now, don't you?'

Steep's eyes opened wide as he stared at Dan. 'Quint! Quint!'

He said nothing more because Mandy shot him through the bridge of his nose. Mandy turned against the doorway and gagged but nothing was left to flow out.

Dan holstered the Peacemaker. He slid down off the desk to his knees. The fire had started to eat up Steep's foot with a flesh-burning smell. Dan's right arm went numb with lost feeling. He bent low and coughed from smoke. A playing-card sized pool of blood dropped to the floor under his lips.

Mandy holstered her gun and knelt to him. 'Dan, let's go.'

'Your arm,' Dan said, He wheezed out a breath that didn't come easy. More blood flowed from his lips.

She got her good arm around his back. 'Get your feet under you. Come on.'

From outside, the rapid shooting had stopped. There were no more war-whoops. The Apaches, must have gone, or been killed. Dan could not hear clearly. He felt no more pain through his chest. His vision formed a black wreath around it, like a circled frame

318

around a picture. The wall of the wreath started to thicken, making the picture smaller.

Mandy urged him. 'Dan, come on. We have to go.'

The black wreath closed tighter. 'Ah, Mandy, I'm too tired, girl. Too many times . . . I think it all wore out.'

She pulled at him. 'Come on. I won't listen to that. Don't give up. You made promises you got to keep. You got to marry me. You promised — Washington Territory.' Tears ran down her cheeks. 'Don't do this to me. Not after all the time I waited. You belong to me and you got to stay.'

'I don't think — so . . . ' The wreath thickened once more, windling his vision. He felt liquid inside, as though life had started to flow out of him through the bullet hole in his lung.

She pushed her shoulder under his arm and straightened her legs. 'Help me. Help me. The fire is getting to the door.'

The black wreath stopped closing.

Dan raised his elbow to the desk. He helped push to his feet, leaning heavily on her. He felt tired — old and tired, his body twisted and torn and scarred. He just wanted to sleep. She was so slim he knew she would tumble with his weight. And her arm was shot. They got out the door and leaned against the unburned section of wall to make the back stairs.

The town of Darion was two lined walls of flame. No structure stood. A soldier rode past them when they reached the horses. Dan held the saddle horn on Mesa for quite a while before he garnered the strength to lift his boot into the stirrup. Gritting his teeth against pain that stabbed his chest and ribs, he pushed up into the saddle, bent against the horn, unable to sit tall.

Mandy held Mesa's reins as they rode on out. 'At the ranch, we'll get you in the buckboard. We'll have to go back to Yuma, get some patching done.'

He had no awareness of how they made it. He held the saddle horn bent over, leaking blood on Mesa's neck. Occasionally he jerked with a bleeding cough. Another kind of black eased thick and syrupy through his thinking. He went off into a riverside camp along a mountain trail, a small fire cracking and snapping, his favorite buckskin tied to a nearby pine, Mandy holding tight against him under a wool blanket. He became vaguely aware of getting pulled into the back of the buckboard then the rough bounce of the trail as they moved away from the ranch. He went back to his mountain river camp with Mandy and slept.

31

They didn't start for Santa Fe until March, 1881. Dan's pierced lung never did heal quite right. Mandy's arm was good as new. She didn't care for the scar it left. After seeing the doc in Yuma, the group had headed out to the Sarah D ranch where they lived unmolested by Apaches through the holidays. The Apache gathered all the released cows and continued raids on miners until army soldiers outnumbered them and herded them back to the reservation around Christmas.

No plans were afoot to ever rebuild the town of Darion.

Once the paperwork became legal, Roger Farnsworth paid Mandy twenty-five thousand dollars for the Sarah D mine, plus a contract for ten percent of all money it made. He was not with them on the trip to Santa Fe. He took over at the ranch and stayed behind to run things.

He made it clear he wanted no part of any damned wedding anyway.

Dan carried a hand drawn map of the Arizona and New Mexico territories. From Yuma, they traveled northeast along the Rio Gila through Pima Village and when they approached the Pima Llano Mountains, the trail swung more north on the General Keamnew's route. The going was slow with the old buckboard and likely older gray. The land climbed, rocky and jagged, weather cooled, always with the threat of rain. They camped along the trail knowing the Apache watched them.

As they continued along the trail, they swung down from mountains to skirt Apache reservations and spotted outlaw bands that refused to be corralled, and so far, continued to outride the army. At Fort Webster, Dan discovered they had crossed into New Mexico. He changed to another route along the Rio Grande.

They were on the Santa Fe Trail.

Fort Webster was crowded. According to a Colonel Stuart, the general was off on an Apache political mission and would not return for a week. With all the humanity flowing along the Trail, there was no room inside the fort. Dan and his ladies might camp along the river outside the walls as the squatters were told to do. That suited Dan. Low-ranked cavalry soldiers inside the fort looked at Jenny and Mandy with the same kind of hungry insolence he had seen in the eyes of Dakota prospectors. Men without women scraped the edges off their civilized thinking. Without women, some men reverted to the savage. They must have conjured up many fantasies about a worn-out gunslinger travelling with two beautiful young women chaperoned by an old walrus with a face capable of stopping a sun-dial. Not just his women, any girl from teens to thirties got the same treatment from them.

Many wagons pushed west, crowding

the river banks, the banks bare of much vegetation — cottonwood trees cut down for firewood by destitute hut residents. Dirt, sand, sagebrush and dry prairie grass stretched to jagged hills along the horizon — past sod dugouts built into small rises with Indian and Mexican family lives dominated by laws of opinion laid down by mission priests — and those who heeded the call of the White Man's Burden to bring hostile savage heathens to Jesus Christ and Christianity. Other clay and sod one-room houses stood alone, most with slanted roofs. Mixed among Mexicans were the deprived, downtrodden Pueblo, Navajo and Apache, preyed upon by many on a personal mission. With so little good in their lives, the poor relied on faith.

★ ★ ★

On the map, Dan found a well-used trail along the Rio Grande named, *Lieutenant Cook's Wagon Route* that headed north beside the Santa Fe Trail. It was smooth enough for the old buckboard. They saw few wagons but as always Navajo and Apache watched them. Hundreds of buffalo clustered along part of the Great Plains to the east.

They were now at the edge of the plains and the land spread flat, puddled in rain with jagged hills beyond. Rain washed down as they kept on the route north along the Trail. After Fort Craig, they passed hut villages with crude signs — Don Pedro, Socorro, and along the Jornado del Muerto until they reached Albuquerque in the Rio Grande Valley.

★ ★ ★

Dan found Albuquerque downright civilized. With a population of about 2,000, the railroad came alongside the town. Once part of Mexico meant there were plenty of missions and churches — and priests dictating life laws to the locals. Past the plaza, Second Street had one of three Red Light Districts with two-story brick buildings and adobe houses supplying quick or prolonged pleasure. Young girls beginning and worn women ending the trade, slithered along boardwalk shadows when the sun went down. Like most righteous folks, the citizens of Albuquerque looked on prostitution as moral failure, not crime. At the corner of Romero and Rio Grande, the Centennial Hotel welcomed Dan Quint and his ladies with two rooms.

* * *

Dressed for dinner, Dan wore his dandy, dude suit he'd taken to North Carolina, having had his bath. The ladies wore their finest; even the shapeless gown of Sleepy Sue fit in with hotel guests. Jenny looked small and fragile and complemented the tight waist and bodice of her bright-green dress. Her dark hair was down to the middle of her back, which made her look ten years younger.

But Mandy shined so bright not one gaze from male eyes passed by her without a stare. Her dress was yellow and showed a daring view of her throat. She wore a yellow ribbon around her neck. Her brown-copper hair drawn together at her cute ears and curled down her back. She did not look like a girl — she looked like a woman.

With a feeling of pride and alert awareness, Dan hoped he wouldn't have to fight his way out of the restaurant to keep her by his side. That was how it was when a man escorted a beautiful woman — and Dan had three — well, at least two, but certainly one of outstanding beauty.

As a uniformed waiter escorted them to the table, a handsome young gambler turned from the bar and said, 'Well, *hello.*'

Mandy flashed him a wide smile, 'Well, *goodbye.*' She hugged closer to Dan's arm.

The hotel had somehow found a bottle of Riesling wine. The meal was a steak fillet so tender it could be cut with the edge of a fork. A salad and a baked potato from Idaho came with the steak, smothered in chives and butter.

Jenny's glance darted left and right, through the lobby, at the restaurant table. 'The man with the comment at Mandy looked at me. He knew me. He had the look. Maybe I can't do this. Men travel, and they talk. Maybe I can't get away from it.'

Sleepy Sue covered Jenny's hand with her own. 'We'll do it, honey. Once we get to Sacramento, it won't matter.'

Sleepy Sue's dough face had transformed since she'd hooked up with Jenny. Dan saw it. She looked soft and gentle, and caring, and no question she was devoted.

'Sue's right,' Dan said. 'He was just some stranger.'

Jenny blinked as if holding back tears. 'The past is always there, ready to ambush you. It never leaves.'

Mandy took a sip of Riesling. 'Are you sure you remember where your little girl is?'

'Trudy,' Jenny said, nodding.

Dan said, 'Do you know the father?'

Jenny shook her head.

Mandy glanced at Dan. She turned to Jenny. 'How old is she?'

Sleepy Sue said, 'Seven.'

'Will she be up for the trip?'

Jenny Troup looked around the table, her eyes red rimmed. 'We'll be together. She was five when I left her. I promise you we'll never be apart again.'

'We roll for Santa Fe in the morning,' Dan Quint said.

32

The first week in May, under clear sky they saw the Santa Fe peaks first, still with a dusting of snow on top. They came upon clusters of clay houses and sod dugouts surrounding haciendas. The Atchison, Topeka and Santa Fe railroad strung from Kansas City across Kansas and Colorado, through Raton Pass into New Mexico straight to Santa Fe, then westward. Wagons moved along streets between stores while churches with crosses above sharp-peaked roofs dominated, both in presence and in rules.

Jenny twitched and blinked and squeezed her hands together. She was quiet and nervous. Entering the town, she moved her head as though trying to see everything at once. She wore her plain, blue dress for the trail.

On Mesa, riding next to the buckboard, Dan said, 'You want to clean up
or change?'

Jenny's hands were shaking. 'I . . .
don't know. Dan, I don't know. I just
don't know.'

Sleepy Sue reined in the old gray and
the gelding.

Dan turned to face Jenny. 'We can
get rooms. How do you know where she
is?'

'I got a map. My sister married a
Navajo. They got two kids of their own.
They don't have much money. They
scratch-farm around their sod house. I
sent them some money when I could.'
The words came out clipped, anxious,
without confidence.

Dan nodded. 'We'll clean up, get
something to eat and head on out
there.'

'All of us?' Mandy asked.

Dan turned to Jenny. 'You want us
with you or not?'

Jenny looked at each of them then
locked on Dan. 'You're our leader. I

don't think I can handle the rig by myself. I want Sue with me. Dan, I'm scared. What if she don't know me, or like me, or what if she won't come with me? Is it too much for you and Mandy to come along?' Her hands started shaking again.

Dan nodded. 'All of us then. Let's move along so we can get out there before dark.'

*   *   *

Vegetable greens grew beside fifteen rows of corn in front of the earth and clay house — a box with a slanted sod roof. A room extension had been built on the west side. Window openings held no glass. The whole structure looked no bigger than twenty feet one end to another, including the addition. A Navajo man stood among the corn rows watching them approach. His face held no expression. Two boys about eight and a girl slightly younger ran around the house. The boys looked Navajo, with cotton shirts and buckskin pants and moccasins. The girl wore a yellow calico dress and sandals and brightened the day with glowing, white hair bouncing to her waist. She squealed as the boys caught her. All three stopped and gawked at the approaching wagon and two riders. The boys turned to stare at the girl. They said something that could not be heard at the wagon. The girl started walking slowly to the wagon. Her blue eyes went from face to face. She looked at the three chickens with tied legs in the back of the wagon.

She looked at Jenny Troup.

Jenny climbed down from the wagon. She twisted her hands together and rubbed them up and down the front of her blue dress. 'Trudy?' she said.

The girl cocked her head to the side and squinted up against a setting sun.

The Navajo man moved along the corn to the front door of the hut. He continued to watch them without expression.

A woman came to the door. She wore

a short, buckskin skirt to her knees and white cotton blouse with her shining, black hair tied at her neck. It reached the hem of the skirt. She carried features similar to Jenny, as did the girl. Her light-brown eyes sat in spider-web wrinkles. She had lines on each side of her mouth and around her neck. Her hands looked rough with the texture of bark.

Dan sat on Mesa. No invitation had been offered.

Jenny knelt in front of the girl. 'Do you remember me, Trudy?'

The girl blinked. 'You're my mama, come to take me with you. I been waitin'.'

'Are you ready to come with me?'

The girl nodded. 'I been waitin'. I been waitin' and waitin' forever, Mama.' She looked up at Dan. 'Who are they?'

'Friends of mine.' Jenny leaned forward. 'Trudy, do you have a hug anywhere there inside you?'

Trudy leaped forward and threw her

little arms around Jenny's neck. Jenny clutched at her, kissed her neck and her face, tears wetting the side of the girl's face. 'Oh, my darling girl,' she whimpered. 'We'll be together always now.'

Trudy kissed her mama's cheek and hugged her tight. 'I been waitin' so long I thought you stopped loving me.'

'I wrote you letters, sweetie.'

'That ain't the same as touching you.'

Jenny squeezed her tight. 'No, my love, it isn't.'

The Navajo man walked forward, still without expression. 'Step on down,' he said to Dan.

'Lord, yes,' the woman at the door said. 'Please, come inside, have some coffee.'

Dan swung down from the saddle. He faced the Navajo. 'Them chickens is for you.'

'Obliged.'

'You got yourself a good growing garden here.'

The Navajo walked to the back of the wagon and pulled the chickens. He untied them and set them free to scatter and peck the ground. In a low voice, he said, 'You take away our little girl — you cut out a piece of my family.'

'I know.'

'Cut out a piece of my heart.' His voice broke. 'My woman will take it hard. She will weep for a week. My boys will be sad.'

'That's the way of it.'

'Trudy has been our only little girl.'

'It has to go like this. They're mama and daughter.'

'Does Jenny have a man to help her?'

'She has friends.'

Mandy had swung down from Rowdy and knelt beside Jenny to chat with the little girl, Trudy. Sleepy Sue stayed on the wagon seat, the reins still in her hands. Jenny took Trudy's hand. She and Mandy headed for the door.

Jenny turned back to the wagon. 'Sue, get down from there and come in for some coffee.'

Sleepy Sue sighed. She dropped the reins and with effort, stepped her bulk down from the wagon seat.

Dan watched her as she passed him. 'You aren't losing her, Sue.'

'Sure.'

'Gather the girl to you. Make it the three of you.'

'I'll try, Dan.' She put her hand on Dan's arm. 'Don't you and Mandy go, please. When you're married stick with us, keep us together.'

'I ain't sure about that.'

'Please.'

'Sue?' Jenny called from the house. 'Get in here and introduce yourself.'

When Sleepy Sue had gone into the house, the Navajo man said, 'Congratulations, you get married. You not marry Jenny, do you?'

'Nope, I marry the one too beautiful, the woman too good for me.'

★ ★ ★

The Los Cerrillos Hotel made all the wedding arrangements — the decorated room, guitar music — they even baked the cake. Attending were Jenny's sister, Kate, her husband, the Navajo, Whip, the two boys, Jenny and Trudy and Sleepy Sue. Jenny was Maid of Honor for Mandy.

Dan did the ceremony without a Best Man.

★ ★ ★

It took two days of arguments to convince Sleepy Sue and Jenny that with the little girl they should take the train to Sacramento, not the wagon. The Sierra Nevada would be too rough, even in summer. They sold the old buckboard and the gray. Jenny and Sleepy Sue cried so deep they got little Trudy to start. But they boarded the train and eventually rolled west.

Dan used the gelding for a pack horse. He rode Mesa, Mandy was on Rowdy. It was a fine day the first week of June when Mr and Mrs. Quint rode out of Santa Fe, Dan thinking about those years on the trail when Mandy was a girl, then a woman — now he was happy to be riding for the tall mountains to trail camp with his beautiful, shiny, loving new wife.

He had no idea what waited for them in Washington Territory. It was bound to be something.

We do hope that you have enjoyed reading this large print book.

Did you know that all of our titles are available for purchase?

We publish a wide range of high quality large print books including:
Romances, Mysteries, Classics
General Fiction
Non Fiction and Westerns

Special interest titles available in large print are:
The Little Oxford Dictionary
Music Book, Song Book
Hymn Book, Service Book

Also available from us courtesy of Oxford University Press:
Young Readers' Dictionary
(large print edition)
Young Readers' Thesaurus
(large print edition)

For further information or a free brochure, please contact us at:
Ulverscroft Large Print Books Ltd.,
The Green, Bradgate Road, Anstey,
Leicester, LE7 7FU, England.
Tel: (00 44) 0116 236 4325
Fax: (00 44) 0116 234 0205

THE DARK TRAIL
TO NOWHERE

Harry Jay Thorn

Lucas Santana is a freelance range detective — and a wanted man in some states — who has several aliases; nor is he shy about lining his own pockets in order to finance his Wyoming ranch. When a number of gold coins surface in South Texas, loot from a big heist years back, both Pinkerton and the US Marshals call on his services to find their source. Problem is, Santana's not the only one searching for it — and when a fellow agent is murdered in cold blood, his quest becomes personal . . .

BAD BLOOD IN KANSAS

Tom R. Wade

John Carshalton, late of the British army, returns to the town of Arabella in Kansas to take up a new job as sheriff. It's a peaceful life — until he gets word of outlaw gangs terrorizing settlements along the Kansas-Missouri border. When John is asked by an army officer to pose as a deserter and try to infiltrate whatever kind of force is being raised, he agrees — but is soon caught up in a web of violence and intrigue that threatens to destroy him, and everything he holds dear . . .

WHITEWATER RUN

Caleb Rand

Thinking that being on the run can be no worse than the torment of phoney incrimination and punishment, Billy Finch escapes from the brutal prison of Great China Wash. Riding many miles south, a vengeful search leads Billy to Walnut Bench and its sheriff, Bigg Harmer, who in a serpentine twist of fate is seeking the same man. Billy decides to strike a deal, and joins a posse of hard-bitten gunmen and outlaws with prices on their heads in a thrilling action-packed trip across the border into Mexico.